Sto

ALLEN COUNTY PUBLIC LIBRARY
3 1833 00699 5200

ACPL ITEM
DISCARDED

CIRCULATING WITH THE LISTED PROBLEM(S):
stains in bottom : top corners

BLT MAI 5/8/17

W9-BSA-317

LOCKET

by

OLIVE RAMBO COOK

Illustrated by HELEN TORREY

DAVID McKAY COMPANY, INC.
New York. 1963

LOCKET

COPYRIGHT © 1963 BY OLIVE RAMBO COOK

All rights reserved, including the right to reproduce this book, or parts thereof, in any form, except for the inclusion of brief quotations in a review.

LIBRARY OF CONGRESS CATALOG CARD NUMBER: 63-13179

MANUFACTURED IN THE UNITED STATES OF AMERICA

U. S. 1226094

To

Melissa
Paul *and* Stephen Shaw

ACKNOWLEDGMENTS

For their help the author is grateful to the following persons of Chillicothe, Missouri:

Mrs. Earl Dupy, Mrs. Edgar Reynolds, Mrs. George Van Deventer, Mrs. James L. Francis, Miss Roxie Eaton, Mrs. George Barnhart, Mrs. Henry Haynes, Ross Cooper, Horace Scruby and George W. Somerville, Missouri, and to Mrs. India Abell Litton, Wichita, Kansas; The Centennial Edition of the Chillicothe *Constitution-Tribune,* published September 13, 1937; And to Miss Meta Antisdel of the Mountain View Public Library, Mountain View, California, and Miss Jane Palmer, Editor of *Wee Wisdom,* Lee's Summit, Missouri, and many, many others.

ILLUSTRATIONS

❧ 1 ❧

A SEARCH BEGINS

Serilda Shaw hurried with the breakfast dishes, wiping them quickly and stacking them in the cupboard beside the kitchen table. Then she washed the three-legged iron spider and hung it on a peg by the fireplace. Last of all she scalded the milk buckets and took them outdoors to the rack beside the smokehouse where they would air in the sun.

She stood for a moment, looking north across Grand River Valley to the hills, a slender figure in the gray-linsey dress, brown braids reaching to her waist, blue eyes intent. There was the smell of wild roses and honey locust mingled with the perfume of apple blossoms from the orchard. A wren, perched on the clothesline sang mightily, and even old Grover, the tan-and-white Shepherd dog, rolled and tumbled in the grass like a puppy. It was June 1870 in north Missouri.

Serilda looked at Ma working in the garden and at Grandma and little Bill putting a hen and her new brood of chickens in a coop. Earlier, Pa and her brother Jeff had gone to the south forty to cultivate corn. Inside the house she could hear the thump of the loom as Katie worked on the weaving. It was a busy time.

She turned wistfully toward the pasture where the horses were grazing. She could see Star, her sorrel mare, with Teka, the little six-months-old filly, beside her. Near them grazed Locket, Star's other daughter, two years old and as tall as her mother. Black as a crow, with one white foot and a white star in her forehead. She was as gentle and eager as her mother with all the style and swiftness of Black Chief, her sire, yet with a certain rollicking way that was all her own.

In her mind Serilda suddenly saw Locket in new harness, hitched to a new buggy, stepping high and handsome before a cheering crowd. She glanced over at the old buggy, she and Jeff had found discarded along the road years ago and that Pa had mended. Even with coats of paint it was a shabby thing.

There will never be another horse just like Locket, Serilda thought lovingly, nor another Star, nor even another Teka. They seemed almost like people. Jeff said that was the trouble with Locket, she thought she was folks, shaking hands and trying to follow Serilda into the house. The horses certainly were not shabby.

Serilda frowned as she thought of the basket of clothes waiting to be ironed and the cream to be churned and the endless chores. She took a deep breath of the perfumed air and turned toward the garden. "Ma," she called, "if Katie and I work fast and get the churning and the ironing done, then may we go riding? It's such a springy day!"

Ma straightened up and pushed back her sunbonnet, her

face red from stooping, brown hair clinging damply to her forehead. She looked up in the pasture at the horses, then at Serilda and a smile lighted her face. "Yes, you may go and I don't blame you for wanting to. It is a springy day for sure."

Serilda whirled and ran back to the house, her full skirts flying and pantalets swishing against her ankles. She hurried into the kitchen and took a black cast-iron pan from the cupboard and placed it directly on the coals in the fireplace. Then she put the flatirons in the pan to heat. It would be nice to have a stove like Lisa Denton's and not have to bend over the hot fire on ironing days. The clothes had already been sprinkled, rolled tightly and put in the basket. It was full.

"Katie, you've been at that old loom long enough. Ma said we could go for a ride when we finish the ironing and the churning. It's heavenly outdoors. Let's fix the churn and get things done!"

Katie gave a flip to the shuttle and it flew across the web. "Three more inches and I'll stop. Your Ma is anxious to have this piece of toweling finished. It won't take long to churn, remember the butter came quick last time. Then we can both iron." She pulled the beater toward her, pushed down on the treadles and sent the shuttle back again.

Serilda danced a step and began to sing as she rinsed the stone churn and scalded the wooden dasher.

"Can't get a redbird a blackbird will do,
Can't get a redbird a blackbird will do,

Can't get a redbird a blackbird will do,
Skip-ta-ma-loo my darling."

Then she made up a verse of her own.

"Can't get a gray horse a white horse will do,
Can't get a white horse a bay horse will do,
Can't get a bay horse a black horse will do,
A high-steppin' horse my darling."

Outside near the kitchen door Serilda lifted the slanting cave door that led down the steps to a small rock-walled room. Grandpa Shaw had made it when he and Grandma came from Indiana nearly forty years ago and homesteaded the place. Here fruits and vegetables were stored for the winter and cream and milk and butter kept in the summer. Covered over with several feet of earth it kept an even temperature. Stone jars under a shelf held sauerkraut, pickles, apple butter and wild plum preserves. Bins held potatoes and apples. Even now there were a few apples left in the bin, and Serilda tucked two of them in her pocket as she took the crock of cream and carried it up to the kitchen.

Katie was right, it didn't take long for the butter to come. Serilda lifted the round yellow lumps into a crock and pressed the buttermilk out with a wooden paddle, rinsing the butter with cold water from the well. Then she filled the round butter mold that held a pound and had a raised design of wheat heads on the top. There were five pounds and a little pat over. It looked real fancy. Ma liked it that way. Ma was particular about butter, and not until this spring would she let Serilda work and mold it.

On the long table Katie spread out an old quilt with a sheet over it. It covered the top so that two could iron, one at each end.

"You know what I want?" Serilda asked as she shook out a pillowcase.

"Something to do with a horse." Katie laughed teasingly as she got a hot iron from the fire.

Serilda laughed, too, then her face grew serious. "I want a new buggy like the one we saw at the wagon and buggy factory in Chillicothe. Red wheels and a real leather top! Side curtains to put on or take off and a top that lets down. Katie, it just took my breath and I can't stop thinking about it. Wouldn't Star or Locket look elegant hitched to that?"

"They surely would," Katie said. "Especially Locket, so shiny black and high-stepping."

"Katie, you've made up your mind to be a teacher and Jeff is going to build bridges when he grows up and I want to raise and show Thoroughbred horses. You have to have books and Jeff has to have tools. If I am going to show my horses at their best I have to have a nice saddle and bridle and a buggy and harness. It's a shame to drive Star and Locket to that old buggy. Pa has mended it and mended it and it's been painted, but it rattles and squeaks. It wouldn't surprise me a bit if turning a corner some day it just fell apart. Katie, before the county fair this fall, I'm going to try and figure out some way to get a new buggy."

"But it will cost sixty-five dollars!" Katie set her iron down on the trivet and stared at Serilda.

"I know"—Serilda dampened her finger and flicked the iron to test the heat—"but one time I wanted a Thoroughbred horse and now I have three. If you want something so hard you ache and pray for it, and don't mind working or swapping for it, I believe you will get it. I really do!" She smoothed out another pillowcase.

"If you think you could swap the locket for a buggy I'll give it back to you right this minute." Katie laughed, but Serilda shook her head.

They were silent for a moment, remembering the time when Katie and her family were traveling over the country in a covered wagon and camped at the foot of the hill, down by the river. Katie was riding herd on a bunch of horses her stepfather had traded for, one of them sick and lame. The next day the father was ready to shoot the lame horse, but Serilda coming home from school ran, screaming, and swapped her gold locket for the horse named Star. Now the shining sorrel mare was up in the pasture with her two daughters, all of them Thoroughbreds and only a long scar on the mare's front leg as a reminder of that day.

Serilda looked across the table at Katie, thinking of the time, months after she had traded for Star, when Katie and her family returned to the camping spot at the foot of the hill. They were on their way to join a wagon train in Westport, Missouri, that was starting soon for the Oregon country. Katie was thin and ill with ague and her mother feared for her daughter to begin the long journey over the plains and mountains. She asked the Shaws to let Katie live with them and work for her keep and go to school. Pa had said that Katie could stay and "we will treat her as our very own." Serilda thought of all the good times she and Jeff and Katie and Star had had together. For she loved the quiet, soft-spoken Katie as if she were her sister.

"I've been thinking," Serilda began again, "of some way I could make money to buy the buggy. I believe that bee trees will be the easiest and the quickest. Honey is worth ten cents a pound, and sometimes bee trees have five hundred pounds, or more, in them."

Katie stopped ironing and looked at Serilda. "Your father says bee trees are getting scarcer every year, Serilda. We could never cut down a big bee tree. Jeff and your father would have to help. And you would need barrels to haul it out of the woods and then take it to market. If it were such an easy way to make money, everybody would be doing it." Katie began to iron again.

"A lot of folks did, a long time ago. Grandma said this very road in front of the house was made by wagons hauling honey and they called it a bee trail. Anyway, I'm going to try it." She squared her shoulders and began humming a tune.

It was after two o'clock when the ironing was finished and the dinner dishes washed. It was too late to hunt bee trees, but time enough for a ride. Serilda skipped to the barn lot and gave a shrill whistle. In the pasture, Star and Locket threw up their heads and whinnied. Locket started running, as smooth and easy as a south wind over the meadows, her mane tossing and tail arched high. She came straight to Serilda, Star and Teka following behind.

Locket gave a soft little snort of pleasure as she stopped in front of Serilda and nuzzled her pocket. Serilda stepped aside and held out her hand. "Howdy-do, Locket," she said, and Locket held up her white foot. Serilda leaned over and took the offered foot, then she patted Locket. Next she looked into Locket's brown eyes. "Do you love me?" Locket made a soft rumble in her throat and nodded her head up and down.

Serilda laughed and laced her fingers in Locket's mane and leaned against her. "That's enough for now. You're much smarter than that trick horse we saw in the circus. They'd surely want you if they knew all the tricks you can do."

Star and Teka crowded in. Serilda took a deep breath of pure joy and patted each in turn. She let Star and Locket each take a bite of apple and gave the last to Teka. "We're going riding," Serilda told them, "and maybe find a bee tree. And we'll sell the honey and buy a new buggy to drive at the fair." Locket tossed her head and Star looked wise.

"I'm not sure about a bee tree, but I do know where we can find some ripe dewberries and May apples," Katie said as they bridled the horses and she climbed on Star. Serilda mounted Locket and Teka gave a lonesome whinny as they rode away.

They turned to the right down the long steep hill that led to the river and the covered bridge. The valley was before them, lush and green, with Indian Hill blue in the distance. Grand River, bank-full from recent rains, flowed in from the northeast. Across the river, the road wound through the valley toward the village of Spring Hill.

"I wouldn't want to live anywhere else in Livingston County," Serilda said happily. "At the top of the hill you can see to the edge of the world and at the bottom is the covered bridge and the mill and the dam. Almost always movers are resting for a while at the campsite and folks waiting at the mill to get their grain ground."

"And some of them wait so long for their grist and have come so far, but it's better than the way your Grandma tells about when they used to burn out a stump and grind the grain with a rock. People are surely learning how to do things," Katie said.

Before they were in sight of the mill they could hear the rumble and roar of the rock burrs grinding, and the rush of water through the forebay. A man was carrying sacks of grist from the mill and loading them into a wagon.

Across from the mill and down by the river, there was a covered wagon at the campsite with a cow and horses tethered near. A spiral of smoke from the fire drifted upward and a woman stirred something in a black iron kettle. Two small boys were playing and calling to each other.

Katie gave a little sigh. "Every time I see boys playing I wonder about my brothers. Do you suppose they remember me? Sometimes I feel as if I were an old woman instead of fifteen, it has been so long since I've seen them."

Serilda smiled at Katie. "Of course your brothers remember you, and your Ma writes they are all doing fine. She sounds happy, too, and your stepfather has homesteaded and built a house and has some horses and cows. Katie, you know your Ma is happy about your doing so well in school. You'll see them again sometime. That's for sure!"

They rode on, into the covered bridge, stopping in the middle to listen to the murmur of the water underneath. It was cool and shady and the sound of the mill and the campers seemed hushed and far away.

2

SERILDA MARKS A BEE TREE

It was almost sunup, a week later, when Serilda heard Pa rattle the milk buckets and start for the barn. Upstairs, Jeff was clumping around getting dressed. Dimly she remembered what Pa had said a few days before. "The first hard rain, when we can't work in the fields, we'll hunt for bee trees." Suddenly she was wide awake. It had rained in the night. She shook Katie. "Get up quick, we're going to hunt bee trees." She slipped into her pantalets and petticoat and hurried into her dress.

Ma already had the batter stirred for the johnny cakes and was putting slices of side meat into the skillet. Hominy sputtered in a kettle and coffee steamed in the pot.

As soon as they were seated around the table and Pa had said the blessing, Serilda asked him, "Pa, it rained so hard in the night. Can we hunt bee trees today?"

Pa was a tall broad-shouldered man with dark hair and brown eyes that were full of fun and twinkled when he laughed. Serilda thought he was the handsomest man in the whole county. He took another bite of johnny cake before he answered. "I can't go, but I reckon Jeff can. Be a right nice day. Every bee in the whole creation will be out after honey. Easy to track 'em, white clover's at its best and locust and plum."

"Jim Denton said there were lots of bee trees up around Horseshoe Lake. How about going up that way?" Jeff asked.

Pa nodded.

Serilda thrilled with excitement. She had only been to Horseshoe Lake once.

Ma looked worried. "That's quite a piece, Will. Maybe you'd better go with them."

"Shucks, you could turn these young'uns loose in the woods on a dark night, ten miles from home, and they'd find their way back. Especially if they had Star and Locket to bring 'em." He laughed and shoved back from the table. "I figure the rest of us will go to Chillicothe, been quite a while and we've not had the mail for a couple of weeks. Salt barrel is about empty and I need to get the ploughshare sharpened."

"If we're going to town there is a lot to do," Ma said quickly. "Serilda, you and Katie fix a bite to take with you and some for us, too, then do the dishes. I'll skim the milk and wash the milk things and rid up the house," Ma was already on her way to the cellar. Then she called over her shoulder, "And you girls wear some of Jeff's old jeans. Be hard on skirts clambering through the brush."

It seemed no time at all until they were ready to start. Tib and Tony, the big bay Percherons, were hitched to the new lumber wagon. Pa proud as always with Ma on the spring seat beside him, and Grandma and little Bill on the back seat.

Serilda mounted Star and Jeff behind her was holding Teka's halter rope

Serilda mounted Star and Jeff slid on behind her, holding Teka's halter rope. Katie was riding Locket, carrying the dinner bucket. Grover, sad and mournful, was left to watch the place.

At the foot of the hill the noise from the mill sent Teka into a panic. She hugged close to her mother's side, eyes white-rimmed. Locket, too, pranced a little, but Star walked straight ahead toward the bridge. Teka snorted and refused to enter so Jeff dismounted and pushed and pulled and struggled to get her inside. "Teka's too full of antics. I'll be glad when she's weaned and can be left at home."

"Maybe Star will be, too." Serilda chuckled.

The air was crystal-clear and Indian Hill dark blue against the sky. A redbird flew across the road and a startled doe and her fawn slipped back into the bushes.

Less than a quarter of a mile past the bridge, they left the Spring Hill road and turned to the right on a road little more than a trail. It went almost due north for a couple of miles where it branched, the left fork going up to Girdner school and then on into Spring Hill, the other angling off toward Potter school and the neighborhood of Poosey. Sometimes the treetops met overhead and it was as if they were riding in a green tunnel.

They had gone nearly a mile when Jeff spotted a tall, dead sycamore up ahead. "Let's tie up there and work over toward the river and follow along that till we come to the lake."

Katie sniffed. "I smell locust blossoms."

"And I smell plum blossoms, too." Serilda threw back her head and took a long, deep breath. "No wonder honey tastes so good when it's made from sweet-smelling stuff like that."

The sycamore was back a way from the road and they tied the horses near it to an oak tree with thick shade and a soft carpet of dead leaves underneath. Teka was turned loose, for she would not stray far from her mother.

The trees were tall with thickets of brush beneath them. Serilda led off and they soon found their way to the locust, its branches full of long hanging bunches of cream-colored flowers. The air was alive with bees, darting from flower to flower.

"I can't tell whether they're going or coming," Serilda said in bewilderment.

"We'll have to get farther away," Jeff said, "and take different sides." So they separated. Serilda stood perfectly still and looked up through the branches into the sky. Bees were darting back and forth and, as she watched intently, they seemed to follow a path across an open space. A prickly excitement swept over her.

"Jeff! Katie! Come quick! I've found the way they're going. It's northeast toward the river. See?" She pointed toward the darting bees.

Jeff squinted up at the sky, then he stepped out into an open spot and looked at the sun and took his bearings. Serilda and Katie walked behind him, trying to keep the line of bees in sight. The ground was soft from the rain and it was hard going. Twice they stopped to rest.

Finally Jeff held up his hand and pointed toward the river.

They froze, motionless, looking the way Jeff pointed. In the stillness they heard a high-sounding hum like a plucked string that never stopped sounding. It was an eerie sound. Serilda felt a little chill run down her back.

"It's bees! It sure is! We've found a bee tree!" Jeff grinned triumphantly and started toward the humming. Serilda and Katie hurried to keep up, struggling through the bushes. As they got closer the hum increased until it was as strong as the keening of a wind.

"It must be a real whopper to sound that loud." Jeff panted as they scrambled over briars and around the trees. Then they saw it. An old hollow sycamore on the bank of the river. Fifteen feet above their heads, a steady stream of bees was going in and out of a hole in the trunk.

"I'll bet it has five hundred pounds!" Serilda was jubilant, already seeing Locket hitched to the red-wheeled buggy. "Jeff, give me your knife and I'll put my X on it right this minute."

"At ten cents a pound that would be fifty dollars. Serilda, that will almost buy the buggy!" Jeff fished his knife out of his jeans and handed it to Serilda.

Serilda started around the tree to find the best place. Suddenly she cried out, "It's already marked!" She pointed to the newly cut X and underneath the initials JD. "It's Jim Denton's."

"So that's why he knew there were lots of bee trees," Jeff said slowly. "I wonder how many more he marked." He sighed and sat down on a log.

"It just happened you found it, too," Katie said, trying to sound cheerful. "It would be a terrible job to lug the honey out to the road."

"He'll shape up the tree and float it down the river to the sandbar by the bridge and haul it from there. Not much of a job," Jeff said glumly.

Serilda sat down on the log by Jeff and Katie. Of all the bee trees in Grand River bottom why did she find the one that Jim Denton had marked. She slapped angrily at a mosquito on her wrist. They sat for several minutes without talking. Finally Serilda got up.

"We can't sit here all day. Let's go on. Jim Denton couldn't mark every bee tree. Maybe we'll find one even bigger," she said doggedly.

Jeff sighed and got up. He looked at the sun. "It's nearly eleven now. We came a mile or more. Let's not get too far from the river."

They trudged along, spread out, but still in seeing distance. Suddenly Katie stopped. "I smell wild plum." They all stopped and sniffed the air. It was a lovely smell. They hurried ahead and came to the little plum thicket, white with bloom and buzzing with bees. It wasn't a moment before Jeff called out, "They're going this way. Come on!"

"I hope it's another big one," Serilda said wearily as they struggled through the brush and around the trees. Once they lost the trail and had to go back, but finally they found the tree, a little dead oak, scarcely a foot through and high up in the trunk a stream of bees going in and out.

"Take a dozen of these to get your buggy," Jeff said as he handed Serilda his knife. "Won't have more'n five or six gallons in it."

"Well, I'm going to mark it anyway. If we find plenty

without it I'll just forget it," and Serilda began to make an S. It took quite a while to mark and Jeff was getting hungry.

"Let's find a log to sit on and eat dinner. It's way past noon and I'm empty clear to my shoes." He picked up the dinner bucket and set off in a hurry.

Logs suddenly seemed scarce and they were about to settle for a grassy spot when they spied a fallen cottonwood up ahead. Serilda suddenly stopped and threw up her hands. "Listen! I hear bees! Millions of bees!"

"It's the log. It's full of bees!" Jeff said in amazement. Then a wide grin spread over his face. "And it won't have to be chopped down!"

They went as close as they dared, but no mark could be seen. Bees buzzed angrily.

"It's a mean swarm, that's why nobody's marked it." Jeff backed off and dodged as one came at him.

"Well, I'm going to mark it, mean or not," Serilda said determinedly. "Give me your bandana and I'll tie it over my head and leave a hole to see out."

"You want I should mark it?" Jeff questioned.

"No, it's me that wants the honey," Serilda said.

"There's a clean rag in the dinner bucket. Let's tear that in strips and tie down your jeans," Katie said.

"And I'll take off my shirt and you can put it on backwards. Pa did that once." Jeff started to unbutton his shirt, then he stopped. "Let's eat first. I'm starved to death."

They ate quickly, then with all but her fingers covered, Serilda stepped softly to the fallen tree and began carving at the spot farthest from the opening where the bees crawled in and out. The air seemed full of bees, over and around her.

Back under a tree Jeff and Katie watched.

The X was almost finished when she got the knife caught in the sleeve and it fell with a clatter on the log. A bee zoomed against the bandana, then another and another.

Jeff shouted, "Run! They're mad! You'll be stung to death!"

"Remember," Pa had cautioned, "if you're covered, stand still. Don't fight 'em." Now Serilda remembered, her heart pounding. She pulled her hands up in Jeff's long sleeves and held the cuffs together. She stood stone still. She waited what seemed forever behind the bandana. Then Jeff called, "They've settled down, maybe you can finish."

With just a tiny place to see through, Serilda began on the first S, sweat ran down her face and into her eyes. Bees buzzed angrily on all sides, but none stopped. When she had almost finished the second S a bee hit and a swift sharp pain ran up her arm. "Right on my thumb," Serilda muttered as she gave a final dig to the letter. Without waiting to see how it looked she turned and hurried toward Jeff and Katie.

Katie untied the bandana and Jeff took his shirt and put it on. Suddenly he let out a yell and yanked it off again. "There's a bee in it! Stung my back!" He looked so shocked that Katie and Serilda bent over laughing.

"Hold still and I'll get the stinger," Katie said and carefully pulled out the little black barb.

"Next time we'll bring some of Ma's soda," Serilda said ruefully and looked at her swelling thumb.

"We know now why the tree wasn't marked," Jeff said as

they started on. "Bees flying low, not like when the tree is standing and the hole up high."

"Now that you have marked it how are you going to get the honey, Serilda? Sting us all to death getting it out," Katie said.

"And have to carry it to the road. Be a terrible job." Jeff frowned and rubbed his back.

"We'll smoke 'em out if it takes all the rags Ma's got." Serilda looked grimly at her swollen thumb.

Jeff turned toward the sun. "It's near four o'clock. We can't be far from the lake. Let's call off the bee trees for today and go look at something that can't bite."

"All right." Serilda laughed and they started out.

They pushed through the brush until they were at the rim of the water, an old cutoff of the river shaped like a horseshoe. A flock of mallard ducks swam near the shore and three long-legged cranes stood motionless on a sandbar. Pale-yellow yoncipin blossoms floated near them on the still water. Except for the movement around the ducks the water was mirror-smooth. They rested for a while, sitting on the grassy bank, and not talking. It was a different world.

Finally Jeff stood up. "By the time we get home it'll be suppertime and I could eat a piece of hickory bark right now if it had a little gravy on it." He took the lead and Serilda and Katie followed. After a while they came to the road and far away, etched against the sky, were the white limbs of the dead sycamore where the horses waited.

❧ 3 ❧

AUNT MATILDA COMES TO VISIT

Serilda knew the minute she stepped into the kitchen that something had happened. Ma smiled absently as they came in and never said a word. Grandma was over by the window reading a letter and did not look up.

Little Bill broke the news. "Grandma got a letter," he said importantly. "Aunt Matilda's coming clear from Bosting to see us!"

Aunt Matilda coming to visit! Pa's sister who went back east to go to school and stayed to teach.

Suddenly Serilda caught her breath. The locket that Aunt Matilda had sent her and that she swapped for Star! "What'll I do when she finds out about the locket?" Serilda cried out.

"She needn't know unless you choose to tell her." Katie spoke quickly. "You can have the locket to wear every day she's here, if you want."

"Tell her the truth," Grandma said. "No need to be ashamed. Tildy liked horses, too."

"She's got a mind of her own." Pa chuckled. "You'll know if she doesn't like it. I recollect when she decided she was going back east to Normal School and didn't have a copper cent to her name. But she figgered out a way to go and she went. When you get your mind set on something you're a lot like your Aunt Matilda," Pa said teasingly.

"Tell me," Katie said urgently, "how did she ever go to Normal School without a cent to her name?"

Pa smiled musingly. "Some folks from New York state homesteaded up by Spring Hill and one of the children and the woman took sick and the man had chills and fever and it seemed nothing went right for them. So they decided to sell out and go back east. Tilda heard of it and offered to go along and take care of them and help out for her keep on the way. And in a covered wagon, too. Never a lazy bone in Tilda. Pa was clean put out and said if she went she needn't come back. Pa was as stubborn as Tilda."

"But you remember, Will," Grandma spoke quietly, "that your father gave her a twenty-dollar gold piece when she started out to get in the wagon and she turned and kissed him good-by."

"But from that day on, she never mentioned coming back until this letter," Pa said.

While they were gathered around the supper table, Serilda told them about marking the big bee tree and how much honey she thought was in it. Enough for the buggy and maybe enough for the harness. "Pa, do you think I could get the new buggy before Aunt Matilda comes?"

Pa put down his knife and fork and looked at Serilda. "Why, Tilda's coming the first of July and you can't take the honey so soon, white-clover honey won't keep till it's aged a little. You know that. And, Serilda, one bee tree, no matter how big, won't buy a buggy and the little one you marked won't help much. It might take you two or three years to sell enough honey."

"Two or three years!" Serilda gasped. Then she lifted her chin. "Some way or other, I'll have me a buggy long before that," she said firmly. "You just wait and see."

"There'll be lots to do before Matilda comes," Ma spoke up. "My, I do wish we had the new house, but since we don't we'll sure have to clean this one."

"Ma, you just finished the spring house cleaning not a month ago," Serilda wailed.

Ma smiled and Serilda could see the planning look in her eyes. Things would be moved around and scrubbed and polished. And they were, too, until the very day before Aunt Matilda was to arrive.

"I'm glad she's coming tomorrow. I don't think I could hold out another day," Serilda grumbled as she and Katie got ready for bed. "Seems forever since we had a minute to visit with the horses and sit on the rock. Locket will forget every trick she ever knew."

Katie was sound asleep and didn't answer.

Ma had everybody up before daybreak, for the train was due in at noon. She wanted every single thing to be just right. And it was. The cupboard and the cave were full of good things to eat, the house was shining and spotless, and Ma and Pa and Grandma were dressed in their best Sunday clothes. Tib and Tony were shining, too. As they got in the wagon to leave, Ma leaned out. "We'll surely be home by four o'clock and you children be all dressed up and waiting. And, girls, be sure and watch little Bill; don't let him mess up the house." She looked at Serilda. "You'll be careful, won't you?" Serilda nodded.

They went back into the house and sat down and looked at one another. There was no work to do. It had all been done.

Jeff looked around and then grinned. "I feel kinda like I'm visiting."

Serilda giggled. "Mr. Shaw," she said, suddenly prim and dignified, "since you are a visitor how would you like to be entertained with a picnic up in the pasture?"

"It is a pleasant place with a wonderful view," Katie said, smothering a giggle.

Jeff stood up and made a little bow. "Miss Shaw, Miss Briggs, it would delight me very much to be entertained with a picnic in the pasture." Then they all shouted with laughter and little Bill turned a somersault in the middle of the floor.

In a jiffy, Serilda and Katie put bread and butter in a dinner pail, with some molasses cookies and cold fried meat left from breakfast, apples from the orchard, radishes from the garden. Jeff filled a jug with fresh water. They closed the door carefully and were on their way.

Hours later they came back and, when Pa drove into the yard in late afternoon, they were ready and waiting, dressed in their Sunday clothes.

Serilda fingered the little gold locket around her neck as she looked at the stranger riding up front with Pa. Would she be high-toned living in the city for so long? Would she care about the locket? Would she even seem to be a relation?

"Well, here's your Aunt Matilda," Pa said proudly as he handed down a slender, stylish woman in a dark-blue dress, with a little flowered hat. She had a long gold chain around her neck and a gold watch tucked in her belt. She stood for a moment and looked at them, smiling, a twinkle in her brown eyes just like Pa's. Then she hugged and kissed them all.

"Give me a hand with Tilda's trunk," Pa said to Jeff as he lifted up one end and eased it over the side of the wagon. They carried it into the bedroom. Then Jeff took in the valise.

Aunt Matilda looked around the yard. "My, how the trees have grown. And the snowball bush and the lilacs! They're higher than my head!"

They went inside and Serilda was proud of the way it looked and glad for the days of cleaning. Ma was right.

"Everything looks so nice. I hope my coming didn't cause any extra bother," Aunt Matilda said as Ma took her into the bedroom.

"None at all," Serilda heard Ma say, "we're so glad to have you." And it sounded as if she meant it.

While Pa and Jeff did the chores, Ma and the girls got supper. The best white linen tablecloth was spread on the table and set with Grandma's blue willowware plates that she got as a bride. Things had never looked nicer and Serilda decided if folks in Boston could beat this they surely had to go some. And the things to eat looked just as good and tasted even better. After the meal was over and dishes washed Serilda knew by the look in Ma's eyes that everything had gone to please her. They were sitting around talking when little Bill walked up to Aunt Matilda and shyly reached up to touch the long gold chain and to peep at the gold watch in her belt. "Does it tick?" he asked.

"Of course it ticks." Aunt Matilda smiled and took the watch out of her belt, pressed the stem and the lid flew up. Little Bill gasped and touched it gingerly, then his eyes grew big with wonder as she held it to his ear and he listened. Then Aunt Matilda put it back in her belt and turned to Jeff. "I need some help to unstrap my trunk. I want to get out some things I brought."

They came back in a few minutes, Aunt Matilda with a tissue-wrapped package and Jeff carrying a big box.

"Ma, this is for you." Aunt Matilda took a folded piece of soft gray silk material from the tissue paper and laid it on Grandma's lap. "And there's a white lace collar and cuffs inside and all the fixings to make it."

She took the big package Jeff was holding and put it down on the table in front of Ma. "I brought this for you and Will." Pa came over by Ma and everyone drew close while Pa unwrapped it. He lifted it out and set it on the table. A Seth Thomas clock! In a walnut case with a glass door that opened and on the bottom half was painted a little white house with a picket fence and flowers by the door.

"Will, you'll have to fasten on the weights and the pendulum," Aunt Matilda said as Jeff brought another package from the bedroom.

"No wonder that trunk weighed so much." Jeff grinned.

Pa tied on the two iron weights, hooked on the pendulum and carried the clock to the mantel, took the key and wound both sides, set the time exactly by Aunt Matilda's watch and closed the door.

"It's an eight-day clock and strikes the half hours," Aunt Matilda told them.

Ma hadn't said a word, but her face was radiant. Now she went to Aunt Matilda and put her arms around her and kissed her, and suddenly they were both crying a little. Pa cleared his throat and got out his bandana and blew his nose.

There was a real boughten shirt of blue plaid for Jeff and a pearl-handled penknife in the pocket. A shirt for little Bill and a funny little toy dog that growled when you squeezed it. A silk scarf for Katie and a little velvet box for Serilda. With trembling fingers Serilda lifted the lid, and there, on white satin, was a gold bracelet, with a heart in the middle. Serilda could hardly breathe it was so lovely. Carefully she took it out and slipped it on her arm. "Aunt Matilda, I just love it!"

"I thought you would," Aunt Matilda said in a pleased way. "I got it to match your locket." She looked at the chain around Serilda's neck. Suddenly there was not a sound in the room, only the ticking of the clock. Serilda felt every eye in the room looking at her. She glanced at Pa and Ma, and then at Grandma, a terrible sinking in her stomach. She put up her hand and fumbled with the chain.

"The locket, it's not mine anymore," she faltered. "I . . . I . . . I swapped it a long time ago to Katie's stepfather for a . . . a . . . sick lame horse. He gave it to Katie . . . and she lets me wear it . . . sometimes."

"And did the horse get well?" Aunt Matilda asked matter-of-factly.

"Oh, yes! And she won a blue ribbon at the fair! And she had two colts! Aunt Matilda, she turned out to be a Thoroughbred!

"Both colts are registered Thoroughbreds, too," Katie said quickly.

"And Star and Serilda saved my life when I cut my foot," Jeff said earnestly. "And they saved the bridge, too, when the flood came."

"I named the first colt Locket, mindful of how I got her mother." Serilda looked anxiously at Aunt Matilda, praying she would understand.

"Well, it sounds to me as if that were the best swap anybody ever made." She put her arm around Serilda and drew her close. "We must be a lot alike, for I'm sure I would have done the very same thing."

Serilda felt weak with relief, there was no doubt now, she felt related to Aunt Matilda.

The next morning Pa and Jeff left for the fields right after breakfast and Serilda and Katie hurried with their work and then went to the barn to groom the horses. They went over each one until they were shining, even Teka. Then Serilda ran to the house.

"Aunt Matilda, come out and see the horses, they're ready for visitors," Serilda said proudly. "You are to sit down and watch, as if you were at a horse show." So Aunt Matilda sat down on the chopping block by the woodpile.

Serilda had never felt prouder than when she led Star out of the stable, shining like burnished copper, the white star and her white legs as snowy as Ma's sheets. "This is Star, that I swapped for the locket." Serilda led her back and forth, then stopped in front of Aunt Matilda. Star put her back feet together and her front ones and stood square, neck arched and her ears forward, brown eyes alert. Just as if Aunt Matilda was a judge at the fair. Star knew what Serilda wanted.

Aunt Matilda stared in astonishment. "Why, Serilda, I never dreamed she would be that handsome!" She got up and walked around Star and stroked her neck. "I've never seen a prettier horse in Boston!"

"And she can almost fly," Serilda said earnestly. "She's been raced sometime, you can tell."

Aunt Matilda looked at the long scar on Star's leg, and when they told her about it, she shook her head in unbelief.

Then Katie brought out Teka, sidestepping and ready to frolic, shying at Grover, and taking a little nibble of Katie's sleeve. She sidled up by her mother and stared wide-eyed at Aunt Matilda, perking her ears and switching her fluffy brush of a tail.

"This is Teka. Her real name on her papers is Wiwasteka; it's an Indian name meaning Beautiful Woman, and Katie named her. We call her Teka for short."

"She's as pretty as a pocketful of new pennies!" Aunt Matilda looked at her admiringly.

"Just wait until you see Locket," Serilda said as she and Katie turned Star and Teka loose in the pasture.

Then Serilda brought Locket, stepping high, her black coat glistening, her silken mane and tail blowing in the breeze.

"This is Locket, Star's first daughter. She's two years old. When the circus was here two years ago we went to it and saw a trained horse do tricks. When Locket was only a few months old we began to teach her and now she does more tricks than the circus horse. She's extra smart and she's a good saddle horse, too. We'll do the tricks now."

Locket nickered softly as they rolled out the round block made from a section of a tree, and upended it in the driveway. Then Serilda took off the halter, leaving Locket free. They stood for a moment waiting, then Serilda spoke.

"Up, Locket! Up!"

Carefully Locket put up first one front foot, then the other on the block, then slowly one hind foot, then the other, balancing herself. "Now show us how you can turn around!"

Locket fluttered her breath and began to move her feet around on the block. Once she almost lost her balance and Serilda put out a steadying hand and talked softly to her. She made a complete turn.

"You're a good girl," Serilda said lovingly and Locket

stepped down and took the piece of apple Serilda had waiting. Then Serilda and Katie held a long, thin pole waist high. Locket pawed restlessly, watching them, and when Serilda gave the signal she trotted back a way and turned.

"Now!" Serilda said crisply and Locket ran a few steps toward them and jumped high and wide over the pole. Then she returned to the starting place and came again to sail over the pole they had raised to their shoulders.

Aunt Matilda cheered and clapped. And Serilda gave Locket another piece of apple.

Next Serilda and Katie held up a big whitewashed wooden hoop, made from slender hickory saplings. Locket gave a quick high whinny and when Serilda said, "Now!" she stood back a little way, perked up her ears, stretched out her nose, and jumped through the hoop without even touching it. Four times she jumped through the hoop, each time faster and higher than the one before.

"This is the hardest of all," Serilda said. "She has to think hard to do this." She put a hand on each side of Locket's head and looked into the deep-brown eyes.

"Locket, do you love me?" Locket perked her ears and nodded her head up and down. "Do you love Katie?" Locket nodded again. "Well, do you love Aunt Matilda?" Again Locket nodded, then she reached over and nuzzled Serilda's pocket for an apple. But Serilda put her hand over her pocket. "Do you love everybody?" Locket snorted and shook her head violently several times. Serilda laughed and gave her the apple.

"There's one more thing." Serilda smiled delightedly as

Aunt Matilda started to speak, and she and Katie and Locket walked out to the road and turned to come back. They stood side by side, Locket in the middle. Each girl stuck out her right foot and Serilda touched Locket on the right side. Then Serilda and Katie began to sing "Yankee Doodle," clapping their hands and keeping step to the music. And Locket, stepping high, her neck arched, ears forward, tail like a banner, kept step with them. This was the most fun of all, the black filly seemed to say as they marched by the audience on the chopping block.

When they stopped, Serilda gave Locket a whole apple. She turned to Aunt Matilda. "The show's over," she said, and made a little bow.

Aunt Matilda looked from Locket to the girls. "I never saw anything to equal it, not even when I went to the horse show in Boston. And not a whip anywhere." Then Aunt Matilda's eyes twinkled and she laughed. "Serilda, you have my permission if you want to swap your bracelet for another lame horse. Go right ahead." Then Aunt Matilda grew serious. "Tell me, who has the Thoroughbred sire of the colts and how did you get the papers for Star?"

So they turned Locket into the pasture and sat down by Aunt Matilda and told her how Katie's mother got the registration papers from the stepfather and sent them back from Astoria, Oregon. And about Black Chief, the handsome Thoroughbred stallion that belonged to Colonel Thompson and was the sire of Locket and Teka.

"I remember the Colonel. Tall, distinguished-looking and

well educated. He always had a fine horse." Aunt Matilda was thoughtful for a moment.

"Serilda, there is talk Barnum is going to form another museum and animal show. I'll wager he would give you a thousand dollars for Locket right today, if he only knew."

Serilda gasped and her eyes opened wide. Then she looked straight at her aunt. "Aunt Matilda, if I were starving I'd never sell Locket. Not if Barnum offered me ten thousand dollars!"

Aunt Matilda laughed. "Then you'll have to train Teka and sell her."

"Teka! I couldn't sell Teka. She's going to be as smart as Locket." Then Serilda laughed too. "I couldn't part with any of them."

"Then if you never sell a horse and all the mares have colts and the colts have colts and on and on, you'll have to figure out someway to make money to feed all these horses and buy saddles and harness and buggies as the years go by. Ever thought of that?" Aunt Matilda said soberly.

"I'm thinking of it right now and I've already marked a bee tree so I can sell the honey and buy a new buggy. But Pa says it will take three or four big bee trees to do that and a long time, too."

"Your Pa is right. It seems to me you'll have to think of some way better than that to make money." She turned to Katie who had kept so quiet. "Do you like horses, too?"

Katie's face was suddenly radiant, her eyes shining.

"Oh, yes, but I like books better. I want to go to the seminary and get an education so that I can teach. I am studying now so I can take the entrance examination next month to see if I can go to the seminary this fall."

"She's the smartest one at Red Oaks," Serilda said loyally.

Katie flushed with embarrassment. "I'm not any smarter, really. I just study harder," she said quietly. "I don't mind working."

"That's what it takes," Aunt Matilda said, "but it has its rewards, Katie. You'll never regret being a teacher." Aunt Matilda got up from the chopping block. "I don't know when I've been so entertained, but I think we should go back in the house and help your Ma."

Grandma had on her white apron with the wide knitted lace across the bottom that she usually wore for company.

"Tildy, we've decided to have a basket dinner late some afternoon and ask all the neighbors and have Amos Willicks bring his fiddle and have music and singing afterward. Would you like that?"

"I can't think of anything I'd like better," Aunt Matilda said, with a smile at Ma and Grandma.

The basket dinner started a round of invitations with everybody trying to put the big pot in the little one for the schoolteacher from Boston. The family had never had such a gay time. A month had sped by and now the time had come for Aunt Matilda to return east.

Serilda wished she would stay in Missouri and live with them forever.

U. S. 1226094

4

BARRELS OF HONEY

The house seemed strangely quiet the morning after Aunt Matilda left and no one had much to say at the breakfast table. Serilda slowly trickled maple syrup over her bowl of mush. "We had so much fun going places and doing things while Aunt Matilda was here, it's going to be hard to live ordinary lives," she said thoughtfully.

Pa chuckled. "How'd you like to open the bee tree and haul in the honey? That's not ordinary."

"Today? Right now?" Serilda slid out on the edge of her chair.

Pa nodded. "Things kinda slack right now. Be a good time."

"I'm going to tie my pants legs down and wear mittens and cover my head. Pa, they have the meanest tempers of any bees I ever saw." Jeff frowned and took another helping of hominy.

"We'll fix a smoke pot and get some old sumac heads as we go along, that'll hold 'em. Been a good while since I robbed a bee tree, now that we've hives of our own. Serilda, you fix us a bite of dinner to take along. We'll make a day of it. Jeff, we'll hitch up Tib and Tony and load the barrels and buckets. Somebody run out in the pasture and get a gunnysack full of pennyroyal, beats anything to keep the bees quiet. Let's get a move on while it's cool."

With some coals in an iron kettle, rags to make smoke, dinner in a bucket, tin pails to carry honey, mittens, string, soda, butcher knife, timber saw and wooden barrels, they set out on their way. Dressed in Jeff's jeans and shirts, Serilda and Katie rattled around with the barrels and stuff in the back. They waved gaily at Ma and Grandma and little Bill as they started down the hill.

Through the bridge and off on the shady road toward the lake, Tib and Tony stepped solidly, Pa singing "Beulah Land" as they creaked along over the trail-like road.

Past the dead sycamore and on down the road until Jeff thought they were opposite the fallen bee tree. Pa stopped the horses and looked around. "Seems there's an open place back in a way. Carrying buckets of honey a mile could get mighty tiresome." They jolted into the open space and Pa and Jeff unhitched the horses and tied them to a tree.

Serilda was so excited she could hardly tie the strings to hold down her jeans. The new buggy seemed closer every minute. They bruised the pennyroyal and rubbed it on clothes and face and hands.

"No use to cover up until we sight the tree," Pa said as they started. Jeff carried the kettle of coals and led the way, Pa bringing up the rear with the axe and the butcher knife and Serilda and Katie in between carrying the buckets.

Pa made a cut in the side of the tree

They were not halfway when Serilda said, "Stop! Listen! I hear bees!"

"And I see 'em!" Jeff pointed up at a scraggly old cottonwood where a stream of bees were going in and out of a hole twenty feet from the ground. "Sounds like a million of 'em."

"Oh, Pa!" Serilda's voice shook. "Can we get this one, too? Today? This and the other one might make enough to buy the buggy *and* the harness!"

"Better see if it's marked," Katie said.

Serilda walked carefully around the tree. It was unmarked.

Pa squinted up at the tree and at the place where it would fall. "We'll take this one first and save the one that's already down for the last. You young'uns go back and bring all the things we'll need. I'll make a smoke and start cutting."

Serilda started running, but Jeff trudged along. "Better save your breath, you'll need it when we start lugging honey from the down tree."

It was easy to follow the trail back to the wagon, then load up and hurry back. Smoke shrouded the tree and drifted into the top branches. Pa had made a cut in the side of the tree, waist high. They covered their heads and put on mittens. Pa had tied his bandana over his cap and buttoned his sleeves around his wrists, but he chopped bare-handed, chips flying. The hum in the tree grew louder and bees darted around angrily.

"Come on with the saw, Jeff. It'll run through here easy as a knife in soft butter."

Serilda and Katie kept the smoke pot going with sumac heads that made a sharp pungent smell. They choked and wiped their eyes, but the bees kept away. Back and forth the long saw slid in and out and the cut grew deeper.

"Going to have to give us a lot of rides in that buggy to make up for this," Pa teased as they stopped to rest and he wiped his reddened eyes.

"I'll take you around the square forty times," Serilda promised and stirred up the smoke pot.

Then it was done and everyone stood back as the tree fell with a splintering crash! Pa moved quickly and chopped through the shell of the tree where the bees had been going in. He pried out a long strip of the hollow tree and made the opening larger. And there lay the honey, gallons and gallons of it.

Serilda peered through the smoke and a chill of excitement poured over her.

"The knife," Pa said, "and the buckets." He began to cut out great chunks of the honey-filled comb and put it in the buckets. The bees crawled around befuddled, or went deep into the comb far back in the tree. Those flying home were the angry ones.

Serilda picked up a filled bucket and started hurrying toward the wagon.

"Take it slow," Pa cautioned. "Remember we've another tree after this one and it's a far piece."

Back and forth from the tree to the wagon, time after time they made the trip. Pa went the last time and carried two buckets.

"Must be twenty-five gallons," Pa said as he emptied the last bucket into the barrel.

"At ten cents a pound and twelve pounds to the gallon, that's thirty dollars! And the other tree's bigger than this one. I'll have enough for the buggy *and* the harness!" Serilda let out a whoop.

"And not one sting, so far," Katie added.

"We're not through yet," Jeff said darkly, "and I'm starving. Let's eat before we tackle that ornery swarm."

So they ate in the shade of a tree and Pa even dozed a bit as they rested.

Then they were on the trail again, Jeff leading the way with the smoke pot trailing a veil around him. They followed close behind him, for bees scented the honey sticking to the buckets and buzzed around. It seemed farther than Serilda remembered and underneath the mittens and the wrappings it was smothery hot. Jeff's shirt was clinging to his shoulders and Katie stumbled once and almost fell. Even before they saw the log they heard the high-pitched hum, with a keening in it.

"Sounds as if they mean business," Pa said as they halted to listen and look at the fallen log. "Four feet through if it's an inch."

Pa rubbed fresh pennyroyal on his face and slipped on some mittens. "Hand me the smoke pot, Jeff, and I'll go in and chop a hole, then you young'uns bring the knife and buckets." He handed Serilda a smoking sumac head. "And don't run, move slow. Nothing riles a bee like hurry'n around."

They watched as Pa went forward. Quickly he stuffed a

smoking rag in the hole of the tree, then he set the smoke pot down close beside him and began to chop. Suddenly he let out a yelp and brushed at his back.

"It's where his sweaty shirt stuck to him," Serilda said grimly and went to him. She rubbed pennyroyal on his back, then waved the smoking sumac behind him. These bees were going to fight!

Suddenly Serilda felt a hot jab in her own arm where the sleeve stretched tight. She stirred up the smoke pot until her eyes smarted and Pa began to cough. Back and forth the axe swung. Home-coming bees came at them in a frenzy, but at last Pa pried out a long opening and peered inside. He motioned to Jeff and Katie and began to cut out chunks of the comb-filled honey.

"Beats the other tree by twenty gallons." Pa choked as he started to fill the buckets and the trek to the wagon began. But the home-coming bees scented the honey buckets and followed them. Jeff got his first sting and suddenly Katie had two.

"We must do something"—Jeff rubbed his shoulder—"or we'll be stung to death by the time the tree's emptied." He picked up a bunch of pennyroyal and began rubbing it on his shirt.

"It's where our clothes are damp and stick to us," Katie said. She picked up a bunch of pennyroyal and began stuffing it down her back. "Let's wad up the pennyroyal and stick it inside to hold the wet clothes away from us."

"Katie, you're plumb smart. I'll bet it works." Serilda

laughed as they began stuffing their shirts and jeans with pennyroyal.

"Save some for Pa, he's got the worst job," Jeff said as they started back.

Pa was waiting under a tree, two filled buckets beside him, a veil of smoke around him.

"Got two more stings on my shoulder. Put soda on 'em," Pa began. "What on earth have you young'uns done?"

"Pa, we stuffed our clothes with pennyroyal, holds our clothes away from us." Serilda giggled. "Unbutton your shirt and I'll stuff you."

"Well, I'll be a humbug! It will be cooler, too. Let a little breeze through." Pa stuffed some in his jeans around his hips.

"Scratches, but sure beats being stung," Jeff said.

Back and forth they trudged with the buckets of honey, Pa going each trip now and carrying two buckets. Each time the path was tramped down more and made the going easier, but it was nearly two miles, round trip, and it seemed to get longer each time.

"I don't believe this is an easy way to make money, after all." Serilda sighed wearily as they emptied the buckets and started back again toward the tree.

Finally, the second barrel was a third full, but now they walked silently, too tired to talk. The sun settled down behind the tall trees and shadows darkened in the thickets.

This trip Serilda took a long, tired breath as they emptied the buckets. She looked at Jeff and Katie leaning against the wagon. Even Pa's shoulders sagged. Across the river whip-poorwills began to call.

"Let's stop," Serilda said. "We're all worn to a nubbin. If I don't have enough honey for the buggy I'll just figger out some other way to get it."

"Stop?" Jeff straightened up. "We've gone this far, let's scrape the bottom of that old tree if it gets pitch dark." He picked up his bucket and started back.

"I'm right behind you," Katie said, and followed after.

Serilda could see the twinkle in Pa's eyes as he looked at her through the slit in the bandana and she suddenly felt rested and hurried to catch up with Katie.

When they reached the tree, the smoke pot had died down and angry bees darted at them. Jeff stirred up the fire and put on a fresh rag. Suddenly he muttered and grabbed at his face. A bee had stung him on the forehead. One found its way down in Pa's mitten and stung his wrist. Katie and Serilda each got a sting. It was the worst of the trips.

It was growing dusk as they started back from the wagon to get the last load. No one talked as they struggled along the path, buckets catching on the bushes, tripping over roots they were too tired to notice. Back at the fallen sycamore, Pa reached down in the trunk and brought up the last of the honey. "I'll leave enough for them to get a new start." He sighed and straightened up. For the first time there were no angry bees. Bandanas and mittens were taken off and stuffed into pockets.

"It sure feels good to have fresh air again," Serilda said as she picked up the bucket. For the last time Jeff led the way, Pa bringing up the rear. Once an animal crashed in the bushes and went running. Up toward Horseshoe Lake a wolf howled. They stumbled along the dim path, it seemed for miles and miles. Far ahead Tib and Tony whinnied and Pa answered with a whistle. At last they were there, buckets emptied, barrels covered, horses hitched and on their way home.

When they drove into the yard, Ma was waiting with the lantern and Grandma watching from the door.

"Will? Is everybody all right? We've been looking for you home since before dark," Ma called out anxiously and held up the lantern.

"Yes, we're all right, excepting for being plumb wore out and nursing some bee stings. The girls are so tuckered they stopped talking two or three hours ago and Jeff's got one eye swollen shut." Pa climbed stiffly down from the wagon and began unhitching.

Serilda and Katie crawled out of the wagon and Ma shone the lantern light on them.

"We have honey in three barrels," Serilda mumbled. "Maybe enough for the buggy and the harness, too."

"Well, all the honey ain't in the barrels." Grandma looked at them and shook her head. "You're the gaumiest, sorriest-looking folks I ever saw. You'll have to wash up or you'll stick to the bed sheets till you can't turn over."

"I wouldn't mind sticking to a bed sheet for two or three days," Jeff mumbled as he led Tony to the barn.

Serilda could hardly remember washing off the honey and getting into bed.

5

THE HONEY GOES TO MARKET

It was a stiff and battered group that gathered around the breakfast table. Jeff squinted at his plate through the little opening of one eye, took a bite or two, and shoved back from the table. Katie sat on the edge of her chair, her back too sore to lean against it. Serilda's shoulders ached. She looked around the table, Pa seemed the freshest of all. He caught her eye and smiled.

"Are you ready to go to town this morning and market the honey?"

Serilda almost forgot the bee stings. "Of course I'm ready. Shall we take Star so I can bring the buggy home?"

Pa leaned his arms on the table and looked at Serilda. "If there is enough money to buy the buggy we'll tie it on behind the wagon. But, daughter, I wouldn't count on bringing it home today."

"Pa, there's honey in three barrels. There must be seventy-five gallons and that would bring ninety dollars."

"It never pays," Grandma said quietly, "to count your chickens before they're hatched. Most always there's a rotten egg left in the nest."

"But all the eggs hatched this time, Grandma," Serilda declared. "The honey is in the barrels!"

Pa glanced at Ma and got up from the table. Serilda ran to change her dress.

It was a cool morning and Tib and Tony jogged along, their big feet stirring up a cloud of dust that rolled out behind them. Meadowlarks sang and a flock of prairie chickens flew up ahead of them. Pa sang a tune or two and when a quail whistled, Serilda mimicked it exactly. Everytime they went over a rough place, Serilda watched the barrels, though Pa said they were far too heavy to upset. At last they were in town and drove up in front of the general store.

Serilda held the lines while Pa stepped into the back of the wagon. He shoved the barrels to the end, then sprang to the ground and took out the endgate.

"Need a little help, neighbor?" a man called from inside the store and out walked Charley Denton.

"Well bless my soul, you're handy as the tines on a fork. I can sure use a little help, got fifty or sixty gallons of honey," Pa answered.

With grunts and mumblings the barrels were eased to the sidewalk. Tipping them on to the bottom rim, the men rolled them into the store, then to the scales at the back of the room.

Serilda tied the horses and hurried in to stay close by Pa. The storekeeper took off a lid and looked inside. "Real nice honey," he said and weighed the barrel. "Two hundred and fifty-six pounds," he announced and wrote it down on a slip of paper.

Serilda took a quick thought and multiplied in her mind. Twenty-five dollars and sixty cents.

The second barrel was rolled on the scales, inspected and weighed. "Two hundred and thirty-seven pounds." The man wrote again and Serilda multiplied and added frantically. Fifty-nine dollars and thirty cents and another barrel to weigh. She could get the buggy!

The third barrel was rolled on to the scales and the man lifted the lid and looked inside. He frowned. "Can't pay full price for this barrel, too much dirt and trash in it. Use it to make beeswax. Give you three cents a pound."

Serilda and Pa peered into the barrel with shocked faces. It was as the man said, chips of rotten wood, little clods of dirt and leaves were in the honey or stuck to the chunks of comb.

"That must have been the barrel we finished filling after dark and we were plumb worn out." Pa shook his head regretfully. Serilda tried to think, even at three cents a pound there would surely be enough for the buggy. She almost held her breath as the man weighed the barrel. "Two hundred and thirty-two pounds." Serilda figured quickly, even at three cents a pound they could take the buggy home and a tiny bit left over!

The man sat down at a little desk and figured on a slip of paper. Then he read aloud, "Two barrels of good honey, four hundred and ninety-three pounds. Take off seventy-six pounds for each barrel, leaves three hundred and forty-one pounds of good honey at eight cents a pound, makes a total of twenty-seven dollars and twenty-eight cents."

"But it's ten cents a pound!" Serilda cried out.

The man looked curiously at Serilda, then at Pa.

"It's to be her money," Pa said. "She aims to buy a buggy when she gets enough."

"Well, you'll have a right good start. Sorry about the price, but got a letter this week from the buyers in Hannibal and honey dropped two cents." He figured again. "The dirty honey at three cents a pound, subtracting the barrel, comes to four dollars and sixty-eight cents. All told, thirty-one dollars and ninety-six cents." He pulled out a drawer, took out the money and began counting it into Serilda's hand. A twenty-dollar gold piece, a ten-dollar gold piece and two silver dollars. "I'll make it even money, for you were a mite disappointed." He smiled at Serilda.

"I'm much . . . obliged," Serilda managed to say and, without looking up, she squeezed the money tightly, walked out of the store, across the street and climbed up into the wagon. She stared unseeing into the trees in the center of the square and tried to hold back the tears that stung her eyelids. Pa came and put his foot up on the hub of the wheel and leaned against his knee.

"I forgot about taking off for the barrels and then only getting eight cents instead of ten, and one barrel dirty! Half the eggs in this nest were rotten!" Serilda burst out.

"Serilda," Pa said quietly, "you've always been in too big a hurry and not willin' to listen. Takes time to accumulate money. You and Star have won two blue ribbons with the old buggy and it looks about as good as it did last year. I could have bought a buggy instead of a wagon, but we needed the wagon and we can all ride in that. Your Ma and me, we don't believe in going into debt unless it's an absolute necessity. Now, this fall you can pick up hickory nuts and walnuts to sell and add to your thirty-two dollars. You'll get your buggy sooner or later."

Serilda turned over the gold and silver pieces in her hand and took a deep quivering breath. The disappointment was razor sharp. She tried to answer Pa, but the words stuck in her throat.

Pa was thoughtful for a moment. "Daughter, you've got thirty-two dollars, not enough for the buggy, but you could spare a mite to get Katie and Jeff a little present. They worked as hard as you did lugging the honey and Katie took time off from her studying. I've got an errand at the blacksmith shop, but you'll have time to look around. I'll be back in about an hour." He turned and walked away.

Serilda sat very still on the wagon seat, turning the money over and over in her hand. Pa's words cut into her thoughts, and she thought of Jeff at home, barely able to see, and Katie too tired to study. Suddenly Serilda wiped her face and smoothed back her hair. She wrapped the money in her handkerchief and slipped it in her pocket, then she climbed down from the wagon and went to the hardware store.

"I want a real good hammer," she told the clerk. "It's to be a present for my brother."

"This is the best we have in the store," the clerk said as he laid a fine claw hammer on the counter. "Tempered steel head and seasoned hickory handle. Well balanced, got a good heft to it. Last a lifetime." Serilda picked it up and looked it over. She wondered if Jeff would ever build a bridge with it. A lifetime was such a long time. "I'll take it," she said after a moment and paid the clerk a dollar and a half.

He hunted under the counter and came up with a little wooden box with a hinged lid. "Since it is to be a present, I'll put it in a box. I hope your brother likes it."

Serilda knew what she would buy for Katie, for they had seen it in a window the last time they were in town and Katie had sighed and looked at it wistfully. It was at a little bookstore that shared a room with the drugstore.

"I want to buy the *Webster's High School Dictionary* that's in the window," Serilda said to the clerk. "It's to be a present."

"Then I'll get one off of the shelf. The one in the window might have flyspecks on it. The Beaucamps at the seminary say this is the most up-to-date copy they've seen and they teach school and ought to know." He smiled at Serilda and wrapped the book. "It will be two dollars and a half."

Serilda went back to the wagon and put the gifts on the seat beside her. She felt a little better just looking at them, but the ache of not getting the buggy was still heavy in her heart. She caught the tantalizing odor of bananas and looked at the money in her hand. Pa liked bananas and so did the whole family. She hurried across the street to the store. "I want a dollar's worth of bananas," she told the surprised clerk and laid one of her silver dollars on the counter.

The clerk plucked the very best bananas from the stalk and put them in a paper bag. "Have you heard?" he asked, "that we're going to have a circus come to town? Their advance agent was here yesterday making plans. Going to be September third, down south of the railroad tracks in that pasture where they had it the last time. Be a big day for Chillicothe."

Another circus! Serilda thrilled with excitement. She pushed aside thoughts of the buggy. Would the circus have the same trained horse, jumping through hoops and over gates and turning around on platforms? Would there be the same big Percherons Pa loved so well, pulling heavy wagons, trotting for bareback riders? And elephants? And tigers? Serilda went back to the wagon, took a banana from the bag and started to peel it, then put it back. "I'll wait for Pa," she decided.

When Pa came Serilda told him about the circus before he could get in the wagon. "It will be here September third. Pa, do you think Johnnie Creason will come to our house again and offer us tickets for pasting the circus picture on the barn?"

Pa grinned. "Don't know, but we won't have long to wait before we find out."

"There's one thing for sure. They won't have any smarter or handsomer horses than Locket. She knows all the tricks that other circus horse knew and some extra. She can answer questions and keep step to music, too. Their horse didn't do that." Serilda smiled proudly.

"No, but their horse may know some new tricks this year," Pa said as he picked up the lines.

"Pa, I got the presents, a hammer for Jeff and a dictionary for Katie. And I got some bananas, too. A whole dollar's worth. We can have all we want." She reached in and took two from the bag and gave one to Pa. "Don't they smell wonderful?"

"They sure do." Pa peeled the skin down halfway and took a bite. "With that many bananas I reckon Jeff can smell us coming when we're a mile from home."

Serilda laughed. With the circus coming the world looked brighter. She tied the money that was left in her handkerchief and stuffed it far down in the corner of her pocket. Once she looked back wistfully, but there was no shining red and black buggy tied on behind the wagon. Only the empty road with little dust clouds stirred up by Tib's and Tony's feet.

6

AN OFFER FOR LOCKET

Pa was right, three days later a man driving a bay livery team hitched to a spring wagon, came swinging into the yard. It was Mr. Johnnie Creason who had put up the circus bill two years ago. He tied the team and came to the door, hat in hand, a broad smile on his round, ruddy face.

"Howdy! Howdy! Mrs. Shaw! It's good to see you." He shook hands all around. "I am representing Bell's circus again. It's bigger and better than ever before." He settled into a chair. "The parade is half a mile long and Mr. Bell himself leads it on his magnificent Arabian horse." He looked at Ma. "And by your leave, Mrs. Shaw, I'd like to place one of our big, beautiful signs on your barn."

"Mr. Johnnie, do we get free tickets?" Serilda spoke up.

Ma looked sternly at Serilda and her face flushed.

Mr. Johnnie chuckled. "Of course you get free tickets. One for each member of the family to the afternoon show."

"The men folks are in the field, but we heard the circus was coming and my husband said to give you permission to put up the sign."

"Fine! How many tickets this time? Everybody over twelve counts as an adult." Mr. Johnnie reached into his pocket and took out a thick leather wallet.

"Seven. Jeff is thirteen, Serilda fourteen, Katie is fifteen, and Grandma and Pa and me, that makes six adult, and one for a child, little Bill is four."

He counted out seven printed slips and handed them to Ma and she thanked him. "Now, I'll get to work. You young ladies and this fine little lad want to help me?"

Serilda and Katie both jumped up and with little Bill, trailed after Mr. Johnnie. A large roll of paper stuck out of the back of the wagon and Mr. Johnnie laid it on the grass and unrolled it. It was as wide as Serilda was tall and three times as long. Mr. Johnnie peeled off one of the signs and handed the ends to Serilda and Katie. "You lead the way and I ll bring the paste bucket and brushes. All aboarrrrrrrd!"

Mr. Johnnie looked at the place for the sign, then using a long-handled brush he slathered the space with paste from the bucket. The children watched wide-eyed as he took a clean, long-handled brush, draped the sign over it, pushed it against the barn, and in some miraculous way smoothed out the paper in long, deft swipes, up, down and around. In two minutes the sign was smooth and tight against the barn for all the world to see. It was red and white and black.

It was almost as good as going to the circus just to look at it. Clowns, tightrope walkers, bareback riders, lions and elephants dazzled the eye. In the center a black horse, ridden by a girl, was jumping over a high fence, the fence held up by two clowns. At the top in red letters a foot high was:

BELL'S GIGANTIC CIRCUS
CHILLICOTHE, MISSOURI
SEPTEMBER 3, 1870
TWO PERFORMANCES
2:30 P.M. and 7 P.M.
PARADE STARTS AT 11 A.M.
COME ONE COME ALL

"I have a horse can jump a rail as high as that all by herself," Serilda said. "Katie and I trained her after we saw your circus two years ago. She does a lot of other tricks, too. She answers yes and no to questions I ask her. Doesn't she, Katie?"

"Yes, she does, and she marches and keeps time with the music when we sing."

Mr. Johnnie Creason looked from one to the other, then he shrugged his shoulders. "The two of you spin a real fancy yarn, but I've sense enough to know that you don't find horses like that outside a real circus. And not even Sam Bell's got one that answers questions or keeps time to music. You girls peddle your stories some place else!" He picked up the bucket and brushes and started away.

"Wait!" Serilda grabbed his sleeve. "I'll whistle Locket in from the pasture and we'll show you!"

Mr. Johnnie stared at Serilda, his face redder than ever.

"It's the honest truth she's telling you," Katie said flatly.

"I'll give you ten minutes to get her in and show her off. I guess this will teach you girls a lesson. I've got miles yet to travel before sundown."

Serilda whirled and let out a piercing whistle, and from far up in the pasture came back a faint high whinny.

"Please tie your team down the road where Locket can't see them, strange horses might bother her," Serilda called over her shoulder as she ran toward the pasture gate.

When Locket galloped up to the gate, Serilda led her to where Mr. Johnnie was sitting on the chopping block, Ma and Grandma and little Bill watching from the doorstep. Katie was waiting with the pole and hoop. "I got the apples, too," she said, "and Mr. Creason helped roll the block."

Locket nickered softly as Serilda led her over to the block, stroked her neck and talked to her quietly for a moment, then stood aside. "Up, Locket! Up!" she said clearly, and Locket placed her front feet, then her back feet on the block and started turning. The show was on. She jumped the pole waist-high, shoulder-high, and sailed through the hoop three times.

Then came the questions and the answers. For Serilda, Katie, little Bill there were swift, sure nods that she loved them. "Now, do you love Mr. Johnnie Creason?" Locket snorted and shook her head sideways several times. Mr. Creason was leaning out on the chopping block, his mouth sagging open.

Then singing, clapping, stepping high, they marched

jubilantly past Mr. Creason. Locket seemed the proudest of all.

"Golly!" Mr. Creason jumped to his feet. "You sure showed me all right! That filly has more fun than anybody. She's a daisy!" He stood by Locket and stroked her neck. "And not a halter, or bridle, or a whip," he marveled. "Just apples."

Serilda and Katie burst out laughing. "And lots of loving," Serilda said as she laid her cheek against Locket.

"And patience," Katie added.

"Whatever it took, you sure had it. You know if India Bell would see that horse perform, she'd want her right now. She used to drive trick ponies, but this year she rides Princess, that black jumping horse on the sign. She and her father are crazy about horses. I'll have to tell them about this. Now I must hurry." He tipped his hat to Ma and Grandma. "I hope you ladies enjoy the circus." He waved good-by to the girls, took a long look at Locket and tipped his hat to her! "Love, patience, apples," he mumbled as he walked away.

At the supper table Pa looked worried when they told him all about it. "Mr. Bell and his daughter won't be the only ones that Johnnie Creason will tell about Locket. The word will get around. There's been a report of horse thieves in the eastern part of the county. I think until the circus has come and gone, we'll keep her in the barn at night." So Locket stayed in the barn at night and Grover slept in the stall with her to be on guard. Whenever Pa heard an unusual sound after dark, or Grover barked, he took the lantern and went outside.

"I wish I'd kept still and not been so smart to show off Locket," Serilda said to Katie.

"But you can't hide a horse like that forever. Half the fun of training her is showing her off to folks," Katie said as she opened a book. "And Locket loves to show off."

It was a week after Johnnie Creason saw Locket that a strange man and a girl about Serilda's age drove into the yard, tied their team and walked to the barn where Pa and Jeff were working.

Serilda and Katie watched from the door as the strangers shook hands with Pa and Jeff. They looked up in the pasture where the horses were grazing. Then they turned and came toward the house.

The man was as tall as Pa, but heavier and wore his Sunday striped suit, a heavy gold watch chain across his vest. He had a dark mustache and keen dark eyes. The girl looked like her father; her long dark braids reached to her waist. Her blue dress and white pantalets had a city look, her shoes shiny and high-button.

Suddenly Serilda knew. "It's the Bells come to see Locket," she whispered to Katie. A sharp wedge of fear, laced with awe and pride, swept over her as Pa brought them to the door.

"This is Mr. Samuel Bell, owner of the circus that is coming to town," Pa said proudly as he introduced them all around. "This is his daughter, India Bell, who rides horses in the circus. That's her picture on the show bill." She shook hands, too, and smiled, especially at Serilda.

Mr. Bell turned to Serilda. "Maybe you've guessed that we came to see your trick horse. Johnnie Creason told us an impossible story about the filly that does tricks, answers questions and keeps step to music. And that you two girls trained her with love, patience and apples. He swore it was true. That he'd seen her. So India and I made the train trip here from St. Joseph to see this fabulous horse perform. Nothing I love more than fine horses and India likes them as much as I do, maybe more." He stroked his mustache and smiled at his daughter, then turned back to Serilda.

Serilda looked at Pa. He nodded his head, Ma smoothed her apron.

"I'll be glad to have Locket do her tricks. She loves to show off." Serilda looked straight into Mr. Bell's dark eyes. "But Locket is not for sale. At any price."

Mr. Bell smiled a little and said nothing. Neither did India.

Jeff and Katie walked with Serilda to the pasture gate. For a moment Serilda's throat ached so that she could not whistle. Then the high call went out and up in the pasture Star and Locket and Teka started toward them.

"He's made up his mind, Serilda, that he's going to have Locket for his circus. He's slick and smooth outside and iron inside. And the girl's as determined as he," Katie declared. They stood for a moment watching Locket running straight toward them, almost floating; Star and Teka trotting behind.

Katie and Jeff got the hoop and pole and the apples and rolled out the block. Pa carried out chairs for the guests and he sat on the chopping block. Jeff sat on the ground beside them. India Bell hung her straw bonnet on the back of the chair and was leaning forward, waiting, dark eyes intent.

Serilda brushed some dust from Locket's white foot, straightened her forelock, smoothed her mane. Side by side they walked to the block and the show began. Trick after trick she went through without a mistake, then she came to stand in front of Serilda. For a moment they stood, Locket motionless, alert, waiting. Serilda stroked her neck.

"Do you love me?" she asked clearly. Locket nodded her head up and down. "And Katie? And Jeff? And Pa?" Locket loved them all. Serilda reached out and rubbed the slender, shining face.

"Now, do you love Mr. Bell and his daughter India?" Locket snorted and shook her head sideways several times.

"But she would love us if we could pet her and feed her apples!" India Bell burst out. "Oh, Serilda, I think your horse is the smartest I ever saw. No bridle or halter or whip!"

Mr. Bell was looking straight at Locket, fingering his gold chain, a calculating look in his dark eyes. Serilda felt a worrisome pride sweep over her. She tangled her fingers in Locket's mane.

"Now we'll march," she said as Katie came up beside her. Out to the road they walked, turned, lined up and started back, clapping and singing, keeping step. Locket whinnied as she saw Star and Teka watching at the gate, then she seemed to step higher and gayer than ever before. As they marched by the Bells, India was leaning forward, watching every movement, and as they came even with her she stood up and began to clap and sing right along with them. Locket swiveled her ears and Serilda went a few steps and stopped. India hurried to them.

"Oh, Serilda, please let me try to put her through one of the tricks."

"But . . . but . . . she's never done tricks for anyone else." Serilda was shocked.

"Please, the first trick, let me try that. Give me an apple and let her smell it."

Serilda watched, transfixed, as India Bell held the apple under Locket's nose and walked toward the block. Then India put the apple in her pocket and stood in front of Locket as Serilda had done. She stroked her neck. "Up, Locket, up!" she said firmly.

Serilda felt choked. A shiver ran over her and she stood quivering, watching. Locket looked at Serilda, then back to India Bell. She lifted her foot, then put it down. "Up, Locket! Up!" India said again. "Up!" Slowly Locket put her front feet on the block, then her back feet and turned around.

"I knew I could do it," India Bell said with a triumphant look at Serilda. She stroked Locket's neck.

"Give her the apple," Serilda said sharply, her voice breaking. Suddenly she hated India, acting as if Locket belonged to her.

Mr. Bell came over to Locket. He looked at her feet, her ears, her teeth, her eyes, rubbed his hand over her withers, down her back, across her rump, as if she were an old crowbait at an auction. A cold fury swept over Serilda. She took Locket's forelock in shaking fingers and led her to the pasture gate. She stood for a long moment, fighting back the tears, before she turned and went back to the waiting group.

"You've a smart, well-trained filly, Miss Serilda. Johnnie Creason told the truth. I'd like her for our circus. She'd fit right in and India Bell could show her. What will you take for her?" Mr. Bell looked from Serilda to Pa.

"She's not my horse, Mr. Bell. Whatever my daughter decides to do, I'll stick by her."

Mr. Bell looked at Serilda.

"She is not for sale . . . at any price." Serilda suddenly felt weak and went over to stand by Pa.

Mr. Bell sat down in the chair. "I wouldn't say that, Miss Serilda. Everybody has their price."

"We'd take good care of her and love and pet her." India looked pleadingly at Serilda. "And keep her just as pretty as she is now and maybe teach her some new tricks."

"How would five hundred dollars sound to you?" Mr. Bell stroked his mustache and smiled at Serilda.

"It sounds mighty puny for Locket," Serilda said shortly.

"Puny!" Mr. Bell yelped. "That's a lot of money!"

"I know it is. An awful lot, but my Aunt Matilda saw her perform and she said Barnum would pay a thousand dollars for her to show in his new museum. And she's from Boston!"

Mr. Bell's face turned scarlet. "Barnum's a millionaire and I'm not!"

"Papa, let's go. She doesn't want to sell her horse and I don't blame her." India took hold of her father's sleeve, but he shrugged her away.

When he spoke his voice was level and honey-sweet.

"Miss Serilda, you've a fine little horse, but out here in the country you and your family are the only ones who enjoy her. Think how many thousands would see her in the circus. And love her. She's a real show-off, too. She'd like it. And think of all the things you could do with the money. She would get the best of care and India would love her as much as you do. Miss Serilda, I'm offering you a thousand dollars for your filly! Spot cash!" He took out his wallet.

A thousand dollars! Serilda leaned against Pa and he put his arm across her shoulders. A new buggy, new harness, a cookstove for Ma, books for Katie, tools for Jeff, help on the new house. Serilda's mind whirled with what a thousand dollars would do! It was a fortune! She looked at Star and Teka and Locket standing like children by the gate, watching the people they loved so much. Then she looked at Mr. Bell, opening his wallet, India beside him, smiling.

A sob tore at Serilda's throat and her eyes filled with tears. "Mr. Bell . . . I love Locket . . . I can't sell her . . . not even for a thousand dollars!"

Mr. Bell looked at Pa, his dark eyes stormy. "Can't you talk some sense into your daughter. She doesn't know how much a thousand dollars is. Tell her to take it."

Serilda felt Pa stiffen and his voice was stern when he answered. "Mr. Bell, Star and Locket and Teka and any of the colts they might have later are Serilda's to do with as she sees fit. I promised her that." Then he turned to Serilda. "Daughter, Mr. Bell and his daughter India have come a long way to see you and your horse and make an offer. He deserves a better answer than you gave him. Tell him you will think about the offer and let him know."

Serilda felt as if she would choke over the words. "I will think about the offer, Mr. Bell, and let you know," she said huskily.

Mr. Bell got up angrily and put the wallet in his pocket. Pa held out his hand. "Now, Mr. Bell, we don't want you to go away with hard feelings toward us, for offering Serilda a thousand dollars for her horse is . . . is a sort of miracle. We sure are much obliged to you and Miss India for going to all this bother, coming so far and everything. Serilda will think things over."

Mr. Bell shook hands with Pa and turned away. There were tears of disappointment in India's eyes.

Suddenly Serilda ached for India Bell. She wanted Locket, too. She would be good to her. Serilda took a quick step toward her. "Maybe . . . maybe . . . I'll see you at the circus," she said hopefully.

"Maybe," India Bell said, a little catch in her voice and she hurried to catch up with her father.

7

KATIE TAKES EXAMINATIONS

It was the day Katie was to take her examinations to see if she could enter the seminary and, when Serilda awoke, Katie was sitting by the window, poring over a history book.

"Have you been up all night?" Serilda mumbled.

"No, just since it was light enough to read. Oh, Serilda, I'm scared I won't pass."

Serilda swung her feet out and sat up on the side of the bed. She rubbed her eyes and frowned at Katie.

"You'll pass. You know everything in the books. You've learned the dates and rules and worked the sums. Katie, you couldn't fail if you tried." Serilda yawned and rubbed her eyes. "I'll sure be glad when it's all over and your mind will be free to think of something else. You've been studying all summer."

"I'm still not real sure about everything." Katie leafed through the book and Serilda saw her chin quiver. "There's just this one day to take all the examinations. There won't be time to think and ponder. I'll have to know."

"Katie, you've not a single thing to worry about. Pa went with you, and you signed the book and know where to go and what to do, and the principal who gives the examinations knows who you are. Katie, everybody else will be worried just as much as you."

Katie nodded miserably. "I know, but that doesn't help any."

Serilda was thoughtful. "Katie, would you like for me to go along? Would that help?"

"Oh, Serilda, if you only would. I've been dreading going alone."

"Then I'll go. Ma will want me to. And if the principal won't let me stay in the room, I can sit out under the trees. We can take some dinner and eat together at noon." Serilda jumped up and began to dress.

At breakfast Katie was too excited to eat.

"Child, you must eat," Grandma urged. "A body can't think well on an empty stomach."

"Katie's stomach may be empty, but her head isn't. Katie, don't worry, you'll pass all your subjects and the seminary will be right proud to have you." Pa smiled at Katie.

Ma slipped a nice hot corn cake on Katie's plate and put the butter and the honey handy.

Jeff grinned and passed the hominy.

It was half-past seven when Katie and Serilda were ready. Katie in her Sunday blue calico and blue bonnet, Serilda in her red calico and straw bonnet. Katie carried an armful of books and a slate.

"You'd do a heap better to leave the books and slate at home and you and Serilda have a good time driving along. Kind of air out your mind. Then it will be fresh for questions," Grandma said.

Katie hesitated for a moment, then she put the books and slate back on the shelf.

Ma kissed them both as they went out the door.

Locket and Teka whinnied from the pasture gate as they drove away and Star answered, then she settled down into a swinging trot toward Chillicothe.

Prairie chickens whirred up in the pastures and cottontail rabbits made dusty tracks in the road. Morning shadows stretched cool and quiet and there was a faint tinge of autumn in the air.

"Katie, have you made up your mind what you are going to do about going to school? Ride Star and stay home, or take care of the Beaucamp children and stay in town?"

"Last night I decided. I'll stay in town and take care of the children. It would be fun to ride Star, but come winter and bad weather I'd miss lots of days. That would worry me."

"It won't be as if you were going far away. I can come and get you Saturday morning, and take you back Sunday afternoons."

"No, I can't do that. When you work for your keep, that means all the time, even if it is for the principal of the school."

"Pa knows the Beaucamps and he says they'll treat you well and you'll have time to study and you'll get fifty cents extra a week. That's something." Serilda tried to sound cheerful, but a sob stuck in her throat. "Katie, I don't want you to go. I wish you didn't ever have to leave!"

"But I do have to. As my Ma used to say, 'Comes a time we all have to do things that give us a heartache.' And this is the time. I've been extra lucky having you folks to live with . . . and care for me. You're . . . my . . . folks!" Katie's voice broke and she turned back the hem of her dress and wiped her eyes.

Serilda tried to still the ache in her heart. "I 'spose then, there'll come a time when I have to sell some of my horses."

Katie nodded. "Bad as it will hurt, you'll have to do it. Can't expect your Pa to feed them forever."

"But Star earns her keep and Locket will, too, when she's older."

"But ten of them wouldn't," Katie said earnestly. "And having a horse farm, means you have to sell or trade some of them to make a profit."

Serilda looked at Katie. "If you'd been me, would you have sold Locket to the Bells?"

"I'm not sure what I would have done, but when I think of what a thousand dollars would do, I suspect I would have."

Serilda was thoughtful for a while and only the thud of Star's feet and a squeak of the old buggy broke the stillness. Suddenly she laughed. "Grandma said for us to have a good time and instead we've been sorry and crying. Can't air your mind that way. Let's sing, 'Listen to the Mocking-bird,' and you take the alto."

Katie smiled and began. Then came the "Irish Wash-woman." Sometimes Serilda tried to sing bass like Pa and Katie warbled up high. They almost forgot about examinations until they were at the edge of town and had to stop singing.

The seminary was east of the square, a fine two-story building, set in a grove of trees and green grass with seats and benches under the trees.

Serilda tied Star in the shade, smoothed her dress and straightened her bonnet. Katie's face was serious. Serilda took hold of her hand and looked into her face. "You know the answer to every question, but if you do miss one or two it won't be any skin off your nose." She leaned closer and whispered, "Remember, you're wearing the locket. That brings good luck."

Katie tried to smile. Together they went up the brick walk and into the building. The principal met them at the door.

"I'm Katie Briggs, and this is Serilda Shaw."

"Yes, I remember you, Miss Katie, but there is no Serilda Shaw on my list." He looked puzzled.

"I'm not taking it, I just came along. Do you care if I sit in the room? I'll be quiet."

"I'm sorry. No one in the room but the candidates. There is a room at the end of the hall if you care to wait there. But it will be a long time with only an hour off at noon if they have finished the morning tests."

Serilda thanked him, then she turned to Katie. "Take all the time you want. Star and I'll be waiting if it's pitch dark when you get through."

Katie nodded, then she took the pen and foolscap the principal handed her. She was already reading the questions written on the blackboard as Serilda left the room.

The waiting room down the hall had chairs, table and maps on the wall. A small bookcase was filled with books; none of them looked interesting. Serilda sat down where she could see the clock in the hall. It was ten minutes to nine. Other boys and girls came and went into the room with Katie, and now and then Serilda heard the principal's voice, but that was all.

Serilda wondered if Katie's mother in faraway Oregon knew that her daughter was this very day taking examinations to enter the seminary. Katie had written her. She would be so proud, Serilda knew. But Ma and Pa Shaw were proud, too.

Serilda tiptoed to the front door to see how Star was doing, Across the street she noticed a circus show bill with the black horse jumping high over the fence. Johnnie Creason had said this circus was bigger and better than the other one. How could it be any better? Elephants and lions and tigers and the little spotted dog that rode a hoop. And the trick horse that gave her the idea of training Locket, who was then only a gay little colt, six months old! And Locket took to tricks as a calf to clover and now the owner of the circus had offered a thousand dollars for her.

Serilda thought again of what the money would buy besides the new buggy and harness. Added to what Pa had saved, maybe the new house could really be built. Maybe a cookstove for Ma to use instead of the fireplace. A carpenter's kit for Jeff. Pa said he wondered if anybody in the whole state of Missouri had ever sold a two-year-old horse for a thousand dollars. But Ma and Grandma had never said right out what they thought. And Colonel Thompson, what would he say?

Serilda turned these thoughts over and over in her mind. She squirmed in the chair, it seemed awfully hard and she looked at the back of her dress to see if she'd worn a hole in it, sitting so long. She glanced at the clock. It was half-past ten. She gave a long, deep sigh. It was most surprising how much thinking you could get done in a short time when you put your mind to it.

Finally it was eleven o'clock, then at last it was noon. Serilda felt empty clear to her shoes, as she walked to the front door and waited. Others came out of the room and went outside until Katie was the only one left. At a quarter to one, Katie appeared.

"Katie! Aren't you starved? Were the questions horrible? Do you think you passed?"

Katie pushed back her hair and looked at Serilda as if she had just come from a far country. Little beads of sweat stood on her forehead and there were inkstains on her fingers.

"It was that last arithmetic sum that stumped me. I'll never forget it. 'It takes a steamboat fifteen hours to travel upstream from Beeville to Grandberg against the current. A catfish that swims six miles an hour in a lake would require three hours to swim downstream from Grandberg to Beeville. If the current of the water is two-thirds that of the boat, then how long will it take the boat to go from Grandberg to Beeville?' "

Serilda rolled her eyes and threw up her hands. "What was the catfish doing in it? Who ever thinks up such things? Let's eat."

Star was unhitched and fed ears of corn in the back of the buggy. Then Serilda and Katie sat in the shade and ate their dinner. "This afternoon we'll have geography, a composition to write, and spelling and government, but the worst is over," Katie said as they walked back to the building.

It was five o'clock when Katie came out of the room.

"Whew! I'm tireder than the day we lugged honey."

"When will you get your grades?"

"Next Saturday morning. We're to come back here and get our papers, too." Katie gave a long sigh of relief. "I feel so light and free. Getting rid of that load is like shedding long wool underwear in the spring."

"Only you do have to put the long underwear back on in the fall, and you won't ever have to take these old examinations again." Serilda laughed as they climbed in the buggy.

Star felt free, too, and she set out for home at a steady trot. It had been a long day.

8

A TELEGRAM FOR SERILDA

Saturday morning Pa hitched up Star and went with Katie to get her grades and to talk with the Beaucamps. Serilda watched them go, then began washing the breakfast dishes. It seemed to take more than twice as long without Katie there to help. The mush pot had never seemed so sticky or the skillet so greasy.

After the milk buckets were scalded, Serilda took them outside to put in the rack. She stood for a while in the warm August morning and looked far across the valley to the blue hills. Grover came quietly and licked her hand. She turned toward the pasture and looked up at the flat rock and gave a little sigh. It seemed there was never enough time to go there as she used to. It was a favorite place for the horses, too. Locket and Teka were grazing near there now and the oxen and cows not far away. Jeff had taken Tib and Tony and gone to help the Dentons with the last of their haying.

There was a faint haziness over the hills and a few yellow leaves on the elm trees. It would soon be autumn, when all the trees were aflame with scarlet and orange and the wild geese flew overhead toward the southland.

Serilda turned reluctantly toward the house where the weaving waited.

It was afternoon when Pa and Katie drove into the yard. Serilda flew out the door. "Katie! What did you make? Did you pass in arithmetic?"

"Did she pass in arithmetic?" Pa sang out. "I'll say she did. She made over ninety in everything and a hundred in spelling and reading. She and another girl headed the list!" Pa smiled proudly and Katie's face was radiant.

"It's all settled. I'm to live at the Beaucamps for my keep and tuition and they will furnish the books and pay me fifty cents a week. If there's extra company I'm to get a dollar that week. And I'm to have a room of my own and time to study and be just like one of the family. And your Pa asked them if sometimes I couldn't come home on Friday evenings and stay until Sunday afternoon and they said I could."

"If the arrangement works out all right, she's to stay on until she is through and gets her diploma and is ready to teach. Which is the same as done!" Pa said triumphantly.

Ma leaned over and gave Katie a kiss.

"When do you have to go?" Serilda asked as they walked to the house.

"School takes up September sixth, but I'm to go in two days before," Katie said.

"Then you can go to the circus with us!" Serilda grabbed Katie and hugged her so hard her bonnet fell off.

Ma had made Katie two new calico dresses and a blue linsey-woolsey dress, two pairs of pantalets and two new petticoats and Katie herself had woven a blue-and-red-checked shawl with fringe all around and a reticule to match. Grandma had knitted her a wool fascinator and mittens and two pairs of stockings. Katie was ready for school.

It was Monday morning and Pa and Jeff had gone to fix fence on the far side of the pasture when a stranger galloped into the yard, tied his horse and hurried to the door. He knocked loudly. "Ma'am, does a Miss Serilda Shaw live here?" he asked importantly.

Ma nodded. "She's my daughter."

"Well, I'm Oscar Petty from Chillicothe and I got a telegram for her and the folks that sent it want an answer back to them, right immediate. The depot agent said I'd best wait for it, save you a trip to town. She's got to sign her name right here on this receipt, if she can write, but if she can't an X will do, or you can sign for her and put your name underneath. That's what the agent explained to me. Then I'm to hand over the telegram."

"A telegram for Serilda? Are you sure?" Ma said doubtfully. Serilda came and stood beside her.

"Sure I'm sure. Look, it says so right here on the front." He held up a yellow envelope. Serilda read her name and a little chill ran up her spine.

"Where's it from?" she asked.

"The agent didn't say, but if you'll sign right here, then you can open it and we'll know." He held out a stubby pencil and a slip of paper. Serilda took them.

"Don't sign any paper without reading every word,"

Grandma spoke up. "No telling what you might get us into."

"It just says, Received telegram Aug. 29, 1870 and a line for me to sign on." Serilda read it carefully and looked on both sides.

Ma was worried. "I wish Will was here. He'd know what was best."

"Well, if that is all it says, it's the truth, you did receive the telegram this day. Can't be any harm in signing that," Grandma said decisively.

So Serilda signed her name and Oscar Petty handed over the telegram. Katie got a knife and with trembling fingers Serilda opened the envelope and took out a folded sheet of yellow paper. It read:

AUGUST 29 1870
ST JOSEPH MO
7 AM

MISS SERILDA SHAW
NORTHWEST ABOUT 3½ MI
CHILLICOTHE MO

INDIA BELL'S TRAINED HORSE INJURED CANNOT PERFORM STOP WILL PAY YOU FIFTY DOLLARS FOR USE OF YOUR BLACK FILLY LOCKET AT BOTH PERFORMANCES IN CHILLICOTHE SEPTEMBER THIRD YOU TO SHOW HER STOP PRACTICE MORNING BEFORE SHOW STOP SEND IMMEDIATE REPLY TO S W BELL CARE OF BELL'S CIRCUS ST JOSEPH MO.

S W BELL

Serilda read it carefully

"Fifty dollars to show a filly two times!" Oscar Petty's eyes flew wide. "Won't take long to make up your mind to that, will it, sister? Easiest money I ever heard of. Sure beats stump grubbin!"

Serilda looked at the sheet in her hand and tried to speak, but no sound came. Her mouth felt dry as dust. Show Locket at the circus! At Chillicothe, before crowds of people! Fifty dollars added to what she had would buy the buggy!

"Do I have . . . have to answer right now?" Serilda gasped.

"That's what it says . . . immediate." Oscar Petty leaned forward to explain. "And the agent he said collect meant this Bell would pay for it when he got it. So that needn't fret you." He turned to Ma.

Ma straightened her shoulders. "I want no girl of mine mixed up with circus people. No real lady would mingle with them. So the answer is No. Katie get us a piece of paper and we'll word the answer."

"But fifty dollars! I'm no lady, but I'd mingle with most any kind of folks for that sum. Times a man works hard and don't clear that much in a whole year." Oscar Petty looked at Ma as if she'd lost her mind.

"Let's not be in too big a hurry." Grandma spoke up. "Mr. Bell can wait. I think Will should have a say in this, too. It won't take more'n half an hour for Serilda to get him, and Mr. Petty can set and rest a spell. Maybe you'd like an apple, Mr. Petty. They're Maiden Blush and right good this year." Grandma picked up the wooden bowl of apples and passed it to him.

Mr. Petty looked at Grandma and then at Ma, frowned and rubbed his face. "Well, since you put it that way, don't care if I do." He shrugged his shoulders and bit into an apple.

Serilda ran to the pasture gate, but tried twice before she could whistle and bring the horses to her. She slipped a bridle on Star, for she could carry double, and headed across the pasture at a fast gallop to where Pa and Jeff were working, Locket running beside her.

"I got a telegram!" Serilda shouted. "From Mr. Bell for Locket at Chillicothe! At the circus! Fifty dollars!"

Pa and Jeff stared at Serilda.

"Pa, it's the truth and the man's waiting to take the answer back. Collect. Right now! I came to get you!"

"Serilda, settle yourself. Tell me slow and careful what has happened. You're all flustered."

Serilda tried to tell him every word, and Pa and Jeff listened. When she finished, Jeff let out a big long whistle.

"Serilda, you ride back and tell the man we are coming. Jeff will help me load the tools and come right along. Give me time to think."

They were all waiting when Pa and Jeff came in the door.

Oscar Petty stood up and held out his hand. "My name's Petty, Oscar Petty, and I brought this here telegram out to your girl. All in good faith, Mr. Shaw. And I feel bound to take back an answer since it said immediate and collect."

Pa smiled and shook Mr. Petty's hand. "Much obliged for you coming, Mr. Petty. Jeff and me been fixing fence. Driving some new stakes. Right warm this morning. Might as well set again." Pa sat down, too.

Mr. Petty looked baffled as he eased down again. Ma handed the telegram to Pa and the room was prayer-quiet as everyone waited. Serilda felt her heart pound.

Pa was thoughtful after he read it. He looked at Ma and then at Grandma. Oscar Petty moved uneasily in his chair. Then Pa turned to Serilda. "Daughter, would you like to show Locket at the circus?"

"Will, I don't . . ." Ma began, but Pa held up his hand.

"Pa, I'd love to show her if I thought I could . . . in front of all the people. Then I'd have enough money for the buggy and almost half enough for the harness, and some left over!"

"Will!" Ma looked at Pa and Serilda had never seen her so determined. "I don't think it's right to let Serilda mingle with that kind of people. And I'll never agree to her showing Locket nighttime at the circus." Ma's lips shut in a firm straight line.

Oscar Petty cleared his throat. "But ma'am. Fifty . . ."

Ma silenced him with a look.

Grandma spoke quietly. "Mr. Bell and his daughter seemed like real nice folks, polite and friendly and all spruced up. I reckon the folks in the circus are a lot like 'em, and if we knew 'em we'd find 'em real neighborly and God-fearing. Folks are about the same anywhere once you get to know 'em."

"I agree," Mr. Petty said heartily.

Pa looked straight at Mr. Petty and Mr. Petty's face turned red. "Maybe I best go outside and let you folks talk this over amongst yourselves." Pa nodded and Oscar Petty went out and sat down on the chopping block.

Serilda waited, tense as a fiddle string, her mind in a turmoil. She squeezed Katie's hand until Katie squirmed. Would Locket be afraid of the wild animals? Would she run away? Would she forget her tricks with all the people clapping? Would she perform after dark?

Pa frowned and pondered. He turned to Ma. "I don't think you have cause to worry about Serilda being criticized for showing her horse at the circus. I'd be as much against it as you, if I thought so. If Serilda is going to raise Thoroughbred horses and train 'em, it's of no use if she doesn't show 'em. Be same as you making a handsome quilt for the fair and hiding it in the closet."

Pa slid his chair over and put his hand on Ma's knee and they talked so low that no one in the room could hear. Finally Pa straightened up and Ma looked relieved. "We've agreed," Pa said, "for you to show Locket at the afternoon performance only, for half the money. Then we'll come home. Serilda, what do you want to do? It's up to you."

"But Pa, twenty-five dollars won't make enough to buy the buggy! Can't I show her at night, too?"

"Considering everything, we don't think it is best. Now you make up your mind and we'll send the telegram back by Oscar Petty." Pa smiled but there was a firm look about his mouth, too.

Serilda flared with resentment. To have the money for the buggy within reach and then get only half. No one seemed to care if she drove the old rattletrap buggy forever! Then a small thought seemed to nudge her. Hadn't Pa worked hard all day chopping down the bee tree, carrying honey, then to market the next day? And Ma had done the chores when they got home late. And Jeff and Katie lugged honey and got stung by bees. Everyone in the family cared. Serilda's eyes filled with tears. Locket had never performed at night, even at home, and sputtering lights, black shadows, strange voices and smells would be too much. Suddenly Serilda knew.

She looked up at Pa and Ma and wiped her eyes, a smile trembled on her lips. "Locket might be scared at night, but . . . I'd love to show her in the daytime!"

Pa smiled and there was a happy twinkle in his eyes. "Then you word the telegram to Mr. Bell and we'll send it by Oscar Petty."

Katie helped and when it was finished, Serilda read it aloud.

AUGUST 29, 1870
CHILLICOTHE, MISSOURI
NEAR COVERED BRIDGE

COLLECT FROM MR. BELL
S. W. BELL
CARE OF BELL'S CIRCUS
ST. JOSEPH, MISSOURI

ACCEPT OFFER. WILL COME IN EARLY MORNING SEPTEMBER 3, FOR PRACTICE WITH BLACK FILLY. IF SHE ACTS ALL RIGHT WILL SHOW HER AT AFTERNOON PERFORMANCE ONLY, FOR HALF PRICE. THANK YOU.

SERILDA SHAW

"Sounds fine," Pa said proudly.

Serilda folded it carefully and took it out to Mr. Petty. "What'd you decide?" He asked anxiously as he took the paper.

"I'm going to show her," Serilda said, a little frightened.

"By Jiminy! That's good! I was right worrit, but I says to myself, nobody in her right mind would turn down that money. Sister, I'll be right there clappin' for you." He tucked the paper in his pocket, jumped on his horse and galloped out of the yard toward town.

Jeff and Katie came running from the house. "Twenty-five dollars for showing Locket! That sure beats luggin' honey," Jeff grinned admiringly.

"Serilda, I'll help every spare minute and we'll put Locket through her tricks every day. Whoever thought Locket would be in the circus?" Katie was jubilant.

Serilda felt weak from the thought of it. She looked up in the pasture where Locket and Star were standing in the shade of a tree, Teka beside them.

"We're to be in the circus, Locket, and everybody will be watching. We'll have to do our very best." Serilda said the words softly to herself. A quiver of excitement swept over her and a feeling that things would never again be quite the same.

❧ 9 ❧

THE CIRCUS COMES TO TOWN

Even when Aunt Matilda came to visit, things had never been in such a flurry. The next day after the telegram, Jim Denton stopped, coming home from town. He had two copies of the Chillicothe *Tribune* and he gave one to Serilda. "Look what is on the front page. All about you and your black horse going to be in the circus. Serilda, you're a big somebody!"

Serilda opened the paper. She could hardly believe her eyes.

LOCAL GIRL TO SHOW TRAINED HORSE IN CIRCUS

MISS SERILDA SHAW, DAUGHTER OF MR. AND MRS. WILL SHAW, IS TO SHOW HER TRAINED, THOROUGHBRED HORSE, LOCKET, AT THE AFTERNOON PERFORMANCE OF BELL'S CIRCUS, COMING TO CHILLICOTHE SEPTEMBER 3.

MISS SHAW, OWNER OF THE THOROUGHBRED HORSE STAR, IS WELL KNOWN, HAVING WON SEVERAL PRIZES AND BLUE RIBBONS AT THE COUNTY FAIR. STAR WAS ALSO HONORED AT THE OPENING OF THE COVERED BRIDGE FOR

HELPING TO SAVE IT DURING A FLOOD. STAR IS THE DAM OF LOCKET.

A TELEGRAM WAS RECEIVED THIS MORNING BY MISS SHAW FROM MR. BELL, MAKING AN OFFER AND IT IS UNDERSTOOD BY RELIABLE AUTHORITY THAT SHE ACCEPTED.

"Well, Oscar Petty didn't waste much time," Grandma said wryly.

"Serilda, you and your horses are sure making a name for the whole of Livingston County. We stopped by the *Tribune* office and they said they'd had a telegram from Bell to print some show bills telling about you and Locket and to hire a man to put them up around town and in the country. Are you in the parade, too?"

Serilda caught her breath. "Oh, my, I don't know. The telegram didn't say."

"Seems to me that new thing called a calliope would scare the living daylights out of any horse. And horses always act crazy when they smell wild animals. Even my old Prince wanted to run when he smelled that panther we trailed up in Poosey. I tell you, you want to be mighty careful," Jim said as he went away.

A cold fear clutched at Serilda. What if Locket was scared and wouldn't perform after all the writing and bragging in the papers. That would be shameful.

"Katie, let's get Locket and beat on pans and make loud noises as they do in the circus. Get her used to it."

"The wild-animal smell, what about that?" Katie asked.

"After Grover, I don't think she'll mind," Ma said, and wrinkled her nose.

Ma and Grandma sat on the doorstep and were the audience. Katie and Serilda on each side of Locket, marched back and forth in the driveway, Serilda with two tin lids that she beat together, Katie with a big dry gourd with a rock inside that she shook around. At first they made the noises soft, then gradually increased them. After a few practice sessions they were singing at the top of their voices and beating and rumbling like a dozen drums. Ma and Grandma and little Bill yelled and clapped as loud as they could as they passed by. As the noise increased, Locket at first refused to march and shied away from Serilda and Katie, but Serilda stopped and petted her until she grew quiet.

"I sure hope nobody goes by and sees us," Ma said, with a nervous glance out to the road.

"They'd think we needed to be locked up in the corncrib." Grandma chuckled.

Star watched wide-eyed from the barn lot and Teka gave a high whinny, stuck her tail straight up and took out for the pasture. The oxen and cows bawled and huddled together, ready to run over the hill. It was a wild time.

The third day, with all the noise, Locket went through every trick. She trembled when little Bill beat on the lids while she was on the block, but when Serilda talked soothingly, she quieted. Star stopped watching and the stock in the pasture began eating again.

They did not practice the afternoon before the circus. Pa and Jeff washed and scrubbed the wagon and the buggy. Ma made pies, boiled eggs and cooked half a ham, getting a picnic dinner ready for the next day. Serilda and Katie trimmed Locket's fetlocks, her hoofs, combed out her tail and mane and got her ready for the show.

In the morning Pa got everyone up long before daylight, but already wagons and horseback riders were going by on their way to see the circus unload from the train and the tents put up.

Serilda hurried into an old dress and ran to the barn, but Jeff was already there, currying and brushing Locket, the lantern on a peg behind them. Star and Teka were in the next stall.

"She's got to shine, today." Jeff grinned as he rubbed Locket's coat until it glistened. Then his face sobered. "Serilda, it's asking a heap of Locket to turn into a circus horse all in a day, but she's like Star. If she knows what you want her to do, she'll put her heart in it. Unless you get bothered and scared she'll do all right," Jeff said loyally, his blue eyes shining in the lantern light. "I'm taking the curry-comb and brush and the rubrag and we'll dust her off again when we get there. And, Serilda, I put a sack of apples in the wagon last night, just to be sure we didn't forget."

It was light in the east as the Shaws started to town. Pa and Jeff and little Bill sat in the front seat, Grandma and Ma in the back seat with Tib and Tony, and the new wagon shining. Coming along behind, Serilda and Katie were driving Star and leading Locket who pranced along, sleek and trim, nickering when Serilda talked to her.

As they neared town, the teams and wagons grew closer together. Neighbors pointed at Locket and called out to the Shaws. They pointed at Tib and Tony, too, for the big bay Percherons were the finest farm horses in the county. They had been brought from the east and Pa had traded for them several years ago. They could pull more than two yoke of oxen and had won blue ribbons at the fair.

A stranger called out, "Miss, is that the horse that's going to do tricks at the circus?" Serilda nodded and he grinned.

Serilda shivered with excitement. She put a cold hand over on Katie's warm one. Locket lifted her head and flared her nostrils at all the strange disturbing odors. She gave a high whinny and Star and the Percherons whinnied, too.

A trail of dust marked the main road to the circus, but Pa took a back street and went another way. Serilda followed. At the far edge of the circus grounds, the horses were unhitched and tied under a tree. The big tent was already up with several smaller tents in a circle behind it. "You folks stay right here and I'll hunt up Mr. Bell and see what he wants us to do," Pa said and then disappeared behind a tent.

The air was full of strange sounds and odors. Locket moved restlessly, her head high, watching, listening. Serilda stood close beside her, and suddenly India Bell came flying around a tent.

"Serilda! I've been waiting for you!" She spoke to the others and stepped up to Locket and stroked her head.

Locket sniffed her hand and swiveled her ears. "She remembers me," India said proudly.

In a few minutes Mr. Bell and Pa came. Mr. Bell nodded pleasantly. "Good morning. We're glad to see you. And how is the little black filly?" He looked at Locket, then turned to Serilda and was suddenly all business.

"The bareback riders are practicing now and the tightwire performers, but the arena will be cleared for you to go through your schedule at ten. We start the parade at eleven and, Miss Serilda, we want you and Miss Katie to ride with India in her pony cart and lead Locket. The afternoon show begins at two-thirty sharp. We'll be watching you practice and give you suggestions. India, show the Shaws about to see how circus folks live." He tipped his hat, excused himself and hurried away.

"First we'll find Boson," India said. "He's been wanting to see Locket. He looks after all the horses and takes care of Princess, my trick horse that got hurt. He helped me train her." She linked her arms through those of Serilda and Katie and led the way.

They went directly to a small tent. A tall, wiry man had just finished bandaging the swollen front leg of a beautiful black mare.

"Boson, this is Serilda Shaw and Katie Briggs and the rest of the family. Serilda owns Locket, the horse we told you about. She's out back, tied to a wagon, if you'd like to see her. Serilda's going to try her out at ten."

Boson took off a battered gray hat. "Glad to meet up with

you-all. Been wantin' to see that little old filly. India and her Papa says she's a right smart one. And that you two girls trained her after seein' our circus two years ago. Sounds like her owner might be right smart, too."

He picked up a jar of ointment and tucked it in his hip pocket, wiped his hands on an old rag and stuffed it in his other pocket. He gave the bandaged horse a little pat. "I sure hope your filly does herself proud this afternoon. I'll go right now and take a look."

India went up to the black mare. "This is Princess. Isn't she a beauty?" Princess nuzzled her hand and gave a soft whicker. "She sprained her leg when she jumped. Boson says she'll have to rest for several weeks."

Serilda went up to Princess and stroked her neck. The mare looked straight at Serilda, her little ears perked forward, her deep-brown eyes searching, inquiring. "I'm Serilda and I think you're beautiful." Princess gave a fluttery breath and pretended to nibble Serilda's hand. Serilda melted. "Oh, India, she likes me."

"Sure, horses know right off who likes them."

"Is she a Thoroughbred?" Jeff asked.

"Oh, yes, she is registered. Khalifa's a Thoroughbred too. Papa got him last year. He's a real Arabian."

Serilda caught her breath when they came to the stallion Khalifa. Snowy white, sleek and shining, his mane hung thick and wavy and his snowy tail touched the ground. Bold dark eyes looked at them and searched their faces arrogantly. Power and speed were in every line. Serilda knew that underneath the shining whiteness was strength and endurance beyond all other breeds of horses. Katie's book told about them.

"He's not mean or ugly, but I'm not allowed in the stall. No one but Papa and Boson. Papa leads the parade on him and I think he loves him almost as much as me," India said, with a little smile.

They hurried on to the big broad Percherons used to pull the heavy wagons and for the bareback riders to perform on. Pa could hardly bear to leave them. Then came the wild animals in their cages.

They stopped by the dining-room tent, where long tables were set for the noon meal. "First year we've ever lived and eaten on the grounds, always got rooms and meals up town. We like it better this way."

They came to the big tent and stepped inside. Two huge poles held up the top. A broad-backed Percheron was trotting around and around in the ring, and a lady rider, dressed in a short full skirt and long tights, was turning somersaults and skipping rope on the trotting horse's back. At one end of the tent a clown was doing tricks with a little white pig.

"Guess this is where you girls and Locket speak your piece," Pa said. "Serilda, you'll have to talk awful loud to be heard here. Like putting a cover over our whole barn lot."

Serilda looked at the tiers of empty seats, the wires and ropes overhead, the center ring where the gray horse was trotting around and around. A cold, weak feeling washed over her. Why did she ever say she would bring Locket here to do her tricks?

10

A PRACTICE SESSION

Boson had used the rubrag and currycomb and Locket was shining. "Gentle as a lamb, an' purty as they come. An' she ain't nobody's fool, either. You an' me, we're old pardners, ain't we, Locket?" He gave a final shine with the rubrag. "Maybe I better lead her in. Confusin' place the first time."

Serilda walked beside Locket, Jeff and Katie bringing the pole and hoop, India carried the apples. At the opening of the tent Locket stopped and threw up her head, wide-eyed. It was completely empty except for Pa and the family in a little group on the seats.

"Let 'er get used to it," Boson said gently. Serilda stroked Locket's neck and talked softly. Jeff handed her a couple of apples to slip in her pocket. She could feel Locket quiver and her own knees felt wobbly. She looked at Katie, and Katie tried to smile as if they were home practicing in the yard.

Boson handed the halter rein to Serilda. "Lead her around a couple o' times. The pedestal is in the middle and begin any time she seems ready."

Slowly they walked around, past Pa and Ma and Grandma,

"Locket," Serilda said, "up! Up!"

and little Bill laughed and clapped his hands. "Sing and march, Serilda! Sing and march!" Serilda laughed and a little of the tightness left her throat. She put her hand on Locket's side and gradually Locket quieted. Twice more around, then Serilda led Locket to the pedestal in the center. A solid, boxlike affair, wider at the bottom than the top. She let Locket smell the apples in her pocket, then she put a hand on each side of the filly's face and looked straight into the brown eyes. "Don't be scared. We're all here. Just like home." She unsnapped the rein of the halter, stepped back and dropped it behind her. Then she stood straight and slim for a minute.

"Up, Locket! Up!"

Locket lifted one foot, then put it back down.

"Locket," Serilda said clear and firm, "up! Up!"

For a moment Locket stood, then up came the white front foot to rest on the pedestal, then the other, and carefully the hind ones. Slowly she turned around and stepped back down. Serilda breathed a sigh of relief. "Good girl, you're a good girl," she said softly, and gave her a bite of apple.

Quickly a man removed the pedestal and Katie stepped forward with the pole. Locket looked at the pole, pawing restlessly, then at Serilda. The girls stood for a minute, perfectly still.

"Now! Locket, now!" Locket walked back a few steps, and as she turned there was a wild trumpeting that filled the tent. Locket whirled and threw up her head, ready to bolt! Serilda shook, her heart pounded.

"Locket . . . Locket . . . Locket . . . Locket," she crooned over and over like a little song and finally Locket quieted and turned toward Serilda. "Now! Locket! Jump now!" For a moment Locket hesitated then she ran a few steps and cleared the pole. She sailed over the high jump like a swallow.

Through the hoop four times, each one a little faster. Serilda looked across at Katie and they smiled at each other.

Boson took the hoop. "You all doin' fine. Just fine. And so's that little old filly."

Now Serilda laid her face against Locket for just a moment. Then she straightened.

"Do you love me?" came the old familiar question, and Locket nodded her head. Nodded again for Katie and Jeff and India Bell, but when Serilda asked her if she loved elephants, she shook her head vigorously.

They marched, clapping and singing as loud as they could, and Locket bowed her neck and arched her tail, stepping high and keeping time. "This is fun," she seemed to say in every movement of her silken body. When they stopped there was a sudden clapping and cheers from the entry where the circus folks had quietly gathered.

Mr. Bell and India came hurrying forward. He grabbed Serilda's hand to shake it and then Katie's. And Locket held out her foot to shake hands, too. Mr. Bell's eyes widened in astonishment as he gravely shook Locket's foot. "Serilda," he gasped, "did she ever do that before?"

Serilda giggled. "Lots of times. That was the first thing

she was taught. When she sees me shake hands she thinks she has to shake, too."

"She will bow, too," Katie added.

"She will? Then have her bow this afternoon when the show is over and the people clap. And, Serilda, we'll see that the elephants don't trumpet. That's what frightened her a while ago. Now, we must hurry. We want Locket to wear Princess' white halter and . . ." Suddenly a bell clanged. "That's for the parade. It starts in ten minutes!"

Serilda snapped the lead rein on Locket's halter, and with Katie, hurried after India. Boson was waiting with a white leather halter and a white saddle blanket that glittered and shone. He gave Locket a quick rubdown, fastened on the blanket, slipped on the halter, straightened her forelock and handed the rein to Serilda.

Another man stood at the heads of matched sorrel ponies hitched to a fancy pony cart with red wheels and two wicker seats, one facing the back.

"I'll sit in the front and you and Katie in the back," India said and picked up the lines. Serilda and Katie got in the back seat, fixed their skirts and straightened their bonnets. Locket pawed nervously. Clowns appeared, hurrying.

Far away, Serilda heard a voice shout, "All aboarrrrrd! Let's go! Move out!" Wagons creaked, voices called, horses strained, and the line began to move.

"They put us in the middle, away from the elephants and the calliope, so Locket wouldn't be so afraid," India said as they turned into the road that led to the town. Far ahead

Serilda glimpsed Mr. Bell leading the way on the white stallion, black trousers, red coat, high silk hat shining in the sunshine. It was enough to take your breath.

Serilda could feel Katie shaking with excitement. Then the band struck up a marching tune and they were on their way. Two men walked behind Locket carrying signs, turned toward the crowds on each side. The people read and clapped, then looked at Locket. When the parade slowed, Serilda leaned out and read the sign. A painted hand pointed at Locket.

COME AND SEE LOCKET, HOME TOWN HORSE, BORN AND RAISED IN LIVINGSTON COUNTY. THE HORSE THAT ANSWERS QUESTIONS, JUMPS THROUGH HOOPS AND MARCHES TO MUSIC. DOES EVERYTHING BUT TALK. THIS AMAZING HORSE SEEN ONLY AT THE AFTERNOON PERFORMANCE. YOUR ONLY CHANCE!

Serilda felt her face flush as she whispered what it said to Katie. Katie flushed, too. Then the parade creaked on, the horses' feet and the wagons stirring up clouds of dust. Across the railroad tracks, up the main street, around the square, the parade wound its way. Thousands of people from all over the county lined the streets. At the very end of the line came the harsh blasts of the steam calliope playing tunes everybody knew, the first that had ever been in Chillicothe. Locket pranced and sidled when it first began, but quieted when she saw the other horses were not afraid.

"Howwwwdy, Serilda! Howwwwwdy, Katie!" It was Jim Denton. Serilda and Katie waved. Farther on there was another shout. It was Jeff and Colonel Thompson and the Rutherfords. Jeff was eating from a bag of popcorn.

When they got back to the circus grounds, Pa was waiting. "Miss India, you're invited to eat dinner with us. Your Ma has already gone ahead with the womenfolks and it's being spread out now. Seems your Pa is too busy to stop at noon."

India Bell was astonished. "That's the very first time Mama ever agreed to do that! Folks ask and ask, but she never will. Mama seems to think circus folks and country folks are kinda rough. She's so quiet and ladylike. Papa and I just worry her to death. She doesn't like circus life. This is the first time she ever came with us."

Pa looked at Serilda and smiled. Then at India. "I reckon your Ma and Serilda's Ma have a lot in common, that's why they hit it off so well."

Pa put the two spring seats on the ground and the grown folks sat on these. Ma had spread a blue-and-white-checked tablecloth on the grass and set out the food from the baskets. Pa watered the horses and fed them in the back of the wagon.

Jeff had not come, but Pa said not to wait, that Jeff could live on popcorn all day if he had to. In the shade of the big tree, Pa said the blessing and they ate dinner just as if the circus was far away. Mrs. Bell smiled and visited with Ma and Grandma and wanted to know exactly how Ma made the vinegar pie; hers never had a flavor equal to this. And she showed Grandma a new stitch in knitting and praised

Katie for going to the seminary. Said she used to teach school before she married Mr. Bell. You could tell Ma liked her.

Serilda looked up and saw Boson hurrying toward them. She felt a cold shiver run up her back.

"Afternoon everybody. Miss India, your Pa wants you all to show the ponies again, right after the wire walkers. Miss Serilda, you and your little old Locket come after the bareback riders in the spot Princess and Miss India had. That makes you be over and done with before the elephants come in. Mr. Bell thought it might spark things up a little if on that last marchin' piece the band would play kinda soft-like and everybody join in and sing on the last verse. Providin' Locket don't get all bewildered."

"She won't get bewildered, but I might. How'll I know when to go in and where to wait?" Serilda asked worriedly.

"Don't you all worry a speck, Miss Serilda. I'll help that little old Locket in at the right time. Get yourselves all slicked up and ready and wait right here. I'll step out between the tents and motion when it's time to come. You all be watchin'. You folks that's goin' to the circus, better get your seats right now, for it's fillin' up fast. Looks to be the biggest turnout yet." He hurried away, India and Mrs. Bell going with him.

Jeff suddenly came running, his face red and his hair wet with sweat, his shirttail hanging out. "Gosh, I didn't mean to be so late. I'm starving; is there anything left? Serilda, is it time for you and Katie?" He grabbed up the brush and rubrag and began grooming Locket. Pa helped. The girls wiped their faces and hands with a wet cloth, then Ma dusted their faces with a little scented powder that Aunt Matilda had left.

"I'm right proud," Ma said, "I've a different feeling about circus folks since I met Mrs. Bell. She's a real lady."

Locket was soon smooth and sleek, hooves polished, mane and tail brushed, the white halter gleaming on the alert black head. Everything was ready.

"I'll stay with the girls," Jeff said as the family started toward the big tent. "I'm hungry enough to eat a nail, haven't had a thing to eat since breakfast 'cepting three bags of popcorn." He began rummaging in the basket and came up with a chunk of ham and a piece of bread. He stuffed an apple in his pocket.

Serilda and Katie sat tense and waiting on the spring seat, Locket standing behind them. Jeff washed his face, combed his hair and tucked in his shirttail. He was waiting, too.

11

LOCKET GOES AWAY

They could hear the band playing and the muted clapping. Suddenly Boson was there between the tents, motioning them to come.

Serilda tried to still the wild beating of her heart. She talked softly to Locket.

"As soon as the bareback riders come out, the ring will be clear and you'll hear an announcement," Boson said. "Then you girls go in. Katie, one of the men will hand you the pole and the hoop when the time comes. He's right here."

"And the apples?" Serilda said quickly. "We left them with the hoop."

"The apples?" Boson whirled. The man shook his head. "No, sir! I ain't seen no apples. Ain't no bag nor nothin' around here!"

Boson swore. "Get apples from the cook and get back here on the double or you're fired!" His face was red. "They ate 'em. I'd bet my last dollar. Serilda do you *have* to have apples?"

"Here. I have an apple!" Jeff grabbed it out of his pocket

and gave it to Serilda. "There's another in the basket," he turned, running.

The bareback riders filed past and Boson moved Serilda and Katie up to the entrance. Locket threw up her head, snuffed the air, flared her nostrils wide.

A man with a big tin horn stepped to the center of the arena. *"Ladies and gentlemen,"* his voice rang out over the crowd, "you are now going to see one of the smartest, best-trained horses this circus has ever shown. She answers questions, she keeps time to music. She almost talks!

"Ladies and gentlemen, she is almost human! Best of all, the owner and trainer has lived all her life near Chillicothe, and the horse was bred and raised on a farm north of this very town, near the covered bridge. This is the first time this horse has ever been shown in public. We must ask you to refrain from clapping until the show is over. We repeat: *Be very quiet.*

"Ladies and gentlemen. We present to you Serilda Shaw, the owner, and Katie Briggs her assistant, and LOCKET, the *thinking horse!"*

"The apples, one won't be enough!" Serilda cried out.

"I'll send it in when your brother comes. Go ahead!"

Serilda felt stiff with fright, Katie's face was pale. Locket snorted and rolled her eyes as they stepped into the tent. Serilda held the rein tight.

"Smile! Smile!" Boson called softly as they went in. "You're three of the purtiest little old fillies I ever did see, outside of Kentucky! Go in. Show 'em how smart you be."

Serilda couldn't help but smile after that send-off. She

glanced at Katie and she was smiling, too, but Locket wasn't so happy. She pranced and sidestepped and snorted. The tent with people banked to the roof was quiet, but Locket could see and smell all the hundreds watching. It was different from the morning.

Serilda talked to Locket, soft and loving, Katie talked, too, reaching up to put her hand on Locket's neck. Serilda reached in her pocket, turned her head away from the crowd and took a bite out of the apple. She slipped it under Locket's nose and Locket lipped it from her hand. It seemed to quiet her. She turned for more, but Serilda kept the apple in her pocket.

Once around the ring, they went to the center where the pedestal was waiting. Katie stepped back and Serilda went forward. She talked to Locket, let her smell the apple, then she took a long deep breath and unsnapped the rein to the white halter. Locket was free!

It was as quiet as a church.

"Up! Locket! Up!" Locket stood for a moment, hesitating, then her two front feet were on the pedestal, then the hind ones . . . and she turned slowly around. After that came the pole and when she sailed over shoulder high, a gasp went over the audience. When the man brought the hoop, he grinned and slipped Serilda an apple. "From your brother," he said.

Through the hoop four times, each one a little faster. The last one like a flash.

"Talk loud," Katie said softly as Serilda started to question Locket.

"Do you love me, Locket?" Serilda's voice came loud and clear. Locket nodded. "Do you love Katie?" Locket nodded. And she nodded for India Bell, too. Serilda patted her. "Now, do you love elephants?" Locket shook her head violently back and forth. A delighted murmur ran over the audience.

Back near the entrance a horn began playing softly and a drum beat the time. Serilda and Katie took their places and Serilda reached out and touched Locket. They were off. Clapping, singing:

"Father and I went down to camp
Along with Captain Goodwin
And there we saw the men and boys
As thick as hasty pudding.
Yankee Doodle keep it up
Yankee Doodle Dandy.
Mind the music and the step
And with the girls be handy."

So softly you could not tell when it began the audience was clapping, too, keeping time. At the last, the man with the horn called out, "Everybody sing." The audience stood and sang and the horn and the drum kept the beat. Locket stepped high and proud, her white foot flashing, her neck bowed and her tail arched. She was not afraid of noise. She was on parade and she loved it!

When the last note faded away, Serilda and Katie and Locket bowed.

Quickly Serilda snapped on the halter rein and they turned to leave the ring. Then the tent rocked with cheers and yells and clapping. Locket reared at the sudden noise, but Serilda and Katie grabbed the halter and led her out. Boson met them, his face shining. "Golly, you are regular old-timers. You sure done that up brown!"

Outside the tent India was waiting. She grabbed Serilda's hand. "It went off slick as grease! I heard every question. The apple got there just in time, didn't it?" India laughed, her brown eyes sparkling. "Your brother almost flew to the wagon and back." She petted Locket. "Pa went to the office, he wants to see you there."

"I'll take Locket to the wagon and see how the other horses are getting along," Katie said.

Mr. Bell's office was in a big wagon, all gold and curlecues on the outside like the others. Inside, were a desk, several chairs and a small table. A window on the side. Pictures of horses, animals, show bills and clippings from papers lined the walls.

Mr. Bell was sitting behind the desk and as they entered he stood up and shook Serilda's hand. "You did even better than I thought you would." He smiled broadly. "Have a chair and rest yourself." He leaned back and began fiddling with his watch chain. Serilda could feel a tension in the air. It had to be something about Locket. Maybe it was about the pay for this afternoon, but that was not it, for he reached into a drawer and took out five five-dollar gold pieces and handed them to Serilda. "And well earned," he said with a smile.

Serilda thanked him and held them carefully. This was not all he wanted, she could tell.

"Miss Serilda, have you changed your mind about selling Locket?"

"No, Mr. Bell, I haven't changed my mind," Serilda hesitated, "but I have thought about your offer."

"I have another offer to make today. Due to your act we have had the biggest crowd of the season. We show seven more towns between here and Hannibal, then show at Hannibal as long as we can get crowds. I figure, all told, about three weeks. If you will let us take Locket with us and show her in the place of Princess, I will agree to pay you two hundred and fifty dollars. Then return her by train and pay the cost. What do you think?"

Two hundred and fifty dollars! Enough for the buggy and harness and tools and books! She caught her breath!

"I . . . . I don't know what to think. Would . . . would you promise to take good care of Locket?"

Mr. Bell smiled. "Such good care that perhaps you wouldn't mind selling her outright next spring. India will take your place showing her and Boson will be right there."

Serilda sat on the edge of her chair, staring at the gold pieces in her hand, yet not seeing them. A prayer hovered on her lips as she tried to decide. Finally she took a deep breath and looked up at Mr. Bell.

"You can take Locket for the rest of the season, at the price you named, but I want to get Pa, he knows more about business than I do."

Mr. Bell smiled, got up from his chair and shook Serilda's hand. "Miss Serilda, it's a deal. I'll write out a contract. India, run and find Boson while Serilda gets her Pa."

The performance had ended and the crowd was pouring from the tent. Serilda saw Pa and the others walking toward the wagon. She dodged in and out around the people and grabbed Pa's arm.

"Pa! Come and go with me to the office. I told Mr. Bell he could have Locket to go with the circus for two hundred and fifty dollars. We shook hands on it."

Pa looked at Serilda. "Talk slow and tell it straight. What is this all about?"

"But Mr. Bell is waiting."

"It won't hurt him to wait." Grandma leaned forward. "Speak carefully, Serilda, I want to hear, too."

So in a close little group, with the crowd hurrying around them, Serilda told the news.

Pa thought it over. "You're sure, daughter, you want to do this. Things could happen to Locket, remember what happened to Princess, or worse. Don't do something all of a sudden you'll be sorry for."

"I won't be sorry. I've been trying to figure out how to get more money and this is the way. I'll have more than enough to get the harness and the buggy and I'll have Locket, too. It won't be the same as selling her outright."

Pa and Serilda went back to the office. Boson and India were there waiting. They made room for Serilda and Pa.

"Of course Miss Serilda has told you of our agreement.

I've drawn up two contracts, exactly alike, one for each of us. You may read them, then if you agree, we'll all sign." He handed a sheet of paper to Pa and one to Serilda.

Outside, the noise lessened as the crowd started home. The shadows grew long. Serilda read carefully.

"There's no mention about payment if Locket should get killed," Pa said. "Would you be willing to pay the price you offered Serilda, if that should happen? Or if Locket should break a leg and have to be put away?"

Serilda choked, her mouth suddenly dry.

"I'm willing to add that, but in all our travels we've never had an accident like that. Mr. Shaw, we take extra care. Our horses are valuable, too." He turned to Serilda, "Is the contract all right with you?"

Serilda nodded.

Mr. Bell added a paragraph about payment for Locket in case of a fatal accident and Serilda signed, then Mr. Bell. On a line marked Witnesses: Pa and Boson and India signed. Then Mr. Bell folded one of the papers and handed it to Serilda.

"Congratulations, Miss Serilda. May this lead to more happy dealings between us."

Serilda took the paper and her hand trembled. "The same to you, Mr. Bell." She tried to smile around the sudden ache in her heart. In a few minutes Locket might be gone forever.

Pa stood up. "We will be starting home right away. Do you want to get Locket now?"

"Yes, I'll go with you," Boson said.

"And I'll come, too," India put her arm around Serilda. "Serilda, I promise, cross my heart, that I'll love Locket and be good to her, just the same as if she belonged to me. We've a friendly old horse called Susie and we'll put Locket with her. She'll mother her."

Serilda could not speak. The closer they came to the wagon the worse she felt. Locket whinnied when she saw them and Serilda tried to keep the tears back. She said a choked good-by to India and Boson. Then she turned to Locket, laid her face against the shining neck and tangled her fingers in the thick mane. Without a word she untied the halter and handed the rein to Boson.

It was almost dark when they reached home. Teka's thin, high whinny came from inside the barn where Pa had shut her for the day. The cows were bawling at the gate, wanting to be milked and the oxen lowing for water.

At the supper table Pa suddenly looked at Jeff and his eyes twinkled. "So much happened today I almost forgot something. I met Steve Ambrose in the crowd. He's working over at Utica on the new bridge. Wants to get it finished before cold weather sets in. Says he could use another good man for a few weeks. How'd you like to give it a try?"

"Me? Help Steve on the new bridge?" Jeff's face lighted. "You know I'd like it! Pa, what'd you tell him?"

Pa grinned. "I told him I wouldn't exactly call you a man, but you'd make a good helper and you'd be there bright and early Monday morning."

Jeff let out a whoop.

"Where'll he stay?" Ma asked worriedly.

"With Steve and his folks. Jeff, you're to meet two men in Chillicothe early Monday and go out to the bridge with them. Serilda can take you in. Ma, seems our family is dwindling mighty fast. Katie leaving tomorrow and Jeff the next day. Serilda, you'll have to be my right-hand man, and Ma's too."

Later, as Serilda stretched out on the soft feather bed, she gave a troubled sigh. "Katie, I'm all bothered. So much happened today and so fast, I can hardly sort it out. This morning I thought for sure I'd have the new buggy tonight. Now I don't have the buggy or Locket either. What if something happens to Locket? She'll be plain scared to death, riding on the train! And what if she meets an elephant face to face?"

"She will just have to meet it, that's all." Katie reached out a comforting hand. "Boson said he'd tie her right by Susie. Mr. Bell's not going to run any risk having to pay a thousand dollars for a dead horse. She'll be back home in a few weeks, smarter than ever. You did the right thing, Serilda, so don't worry about it." Katie yawned and was suddenly asleep.

Serilda finally went to sleep, too, but her dreams were troubled. She was all alone, driving Star to the old buggy, over a bridge that was not finished. She searched everywhere for Katie and Jeff and Locket, and could not find them. Once she wakened and heard the far-off whistle of a train. It sounded bleak and lonely in the darkness.

12

LOCKET COMES HOME

The next three weeks were the loneliest Serilda could ever remember. Jeff and Katie were gone. Jeff came back for Sundays, but Katie had not been home. There had been a short letter from India saying Locket had settled down and was doing fine. Boson had taught her to do without apples until she had finished marching. A boy marched ahead, playing "Yankee Doodle" on a flute and the people cheered and yelled just as they had in Chillicothe. When Locket was put on the train they would send a telegram when to meet her, probably sometime Friday the twenty-sixth.

And today was the twenty-sixth.

Serilda awoke when she heard Pa putting fresh wood on the fire. She bounced out of bed and flew into her clothes. Just any minute Oscar Petty might come galloping up the road with the telegram.

The chores were all done and breakfast over. Ma and Grandma were busy giving last-minute touches to a new quilt they were entering at the fair. Pa had gone to the cornfield to search out the choicest ears for display along with a huge squash he had brought in from the field last week. The coverlid that had been a prize winner two years ago, was already wrapped, but Lucy Denton said her mother had finished a coverlid that she thought would beat it.

Serilda washed the dishes, straightened the house, looked up the road a dozen times, and finally sat down at the loom and began to weave. It was ten o'clock, then eleven, and Serilda got dinner so that Ma and Grandma could keep on working.

After dinner Pa said he was going to mend fence by the pasture and to ring the dinner bell when the telegram came. Then it was one o'clock, two, and then three. Something terrible must have happened. Maybe there had been a train wreck! At five o'clock Pa came in, thinking he might not have heard the dinner bell. It hadn't rung. There was no telegram.

Serilda felt an aching loneliness as night came on.

"You'll hear tomorrow," Grandma said. "I reckon something happened the Bells hadn't planned on. Just as in a family, only worse in a circus."

"But India said in her letter they would probably send her the twenty-sixth," Serilda said wearily.

"If we don't hear tomorrow, we'll send a telegram to them," Pa promised as he took off his boots for the night.

It was a long time before Serilda went to sleep. The lonely whippoorwills called down by the river. A dog howled, and Denton's dogs took up the cry. Out in the sitting room the clock struck off the hours in the darkness and Serilda thought of all the things that could have happened. She might never see Locket again.

It was ten o'clock the next morning when Serilda heard the galloping hooves and ran to the door. Oscar Petty turned into the yard and flung himself from the saddle. "Another telegram for you, Miss Serilda. Seems you get more o' these things than anybody, but of course 'tain't everybody has a trained horse." He took the telegram from his pocket and handed it to her with a little flourish.

Serilda ripped off the end of the envelope. "Excuse me, Mr. Petty, but I want to know right now."

"That's all right." He grinned understandingly. "I got a hankerin' to know, too."

Serilda read aloud:

LOCKET LEAVING HANNIBAL ON TRAIN NO. 3 SATURDAY AT 5 AM STOP ARRIVE CHILLICOTHE 6 PM STOP LETTER FOLLOWS STOP

S W BELL

Oscar Petty rubbed his nose and peered at the yellow paper in Serilda's hand. "I wonder why they put that STOP between Hannibal and Chillicothe? Don't seem that it rightly belongs there."

Serilda laughed right out. "I don't care where they put it. Locket's coming home."

Oscar Petty smiled, too, and rubbed his nose again. "As I said afore, really 'tain't none of my business," he cleared his throat, "but I been hankerin'. Did you really get the fifty dollars that man Bell promised you in that other telegram?" His sharp blue eyes looked straight at Serilda.

Serilda choked back a laugh that threatened to spill over. She looked square at Mr. Petty, her face sober. "No, I didn't get fifty dollars."

Oscar Petty gasped and shook his head. "I just knew you wouldn't. I don't trust these here telegrams, comin' through the air like they do. Like as not your Locket won't be on the train." He shook his head sympathetically, climbed on his horse and started back to town.

Serilda raced to the dinner bell and rang it hard, so Pa would come. She hurried to fix a bite to eat, whistling a gay tune.

It was noon when Pa and Serilda left for Chillicothe, driving the big bay Percherons to the wagon. "We'll tie the new buggy on behind, if you get it, and you can sit in it and lead Locket. Not right to expect her to pull it after riding all day on the train."

It was a warm fall day. Gold and scarlet were beginning to show in the trees and goldenrod and wild purple asters dotted the roadside. Flocks of geese and ducks were winging their way southward. A soft haze hung like a veil over the blue hills. Nights were cool and mornings crisp. It was the time of year that Serilda loved best.

"Pa, I've been thinking," she said as they drove along, "and last night I decided what I'd like to do with the money Locket earned."

"No need to spend it all," Pa cautioned as he pushed a

horsefly off Tony's back with the line. "Best to save some of every piece of money you make. Your Ma and I always do."

"That's what I want to talk about. Something for Ma. Liza Denton got a cookstove this summer and she likes it fine. Pa, what do they cost?"

Pa chuckled. "I been wanting to buy your Ma a cookstove for a long time, but she wanted every penny saved toward the new house, she craves it so. But one time she did go look at them. I know the one she likes best. And what else?"

"The buggy and the harness, that will take about ninety dollars. And I want to give Katie twenty-five dollars or more to have for her own. She helped to earn every cent. Pa, seems as if I never give you anything, but I'll have some more money from the fair."

"Daughter, when you get more horses, and it takes a lot of feed, then we'll talk about money. It was our agreement that I was to feed them, but you were to buy any bridles or saddles or buggies with your own money. I'll take my share in having a buggy horse to use, or one to ride when I need it. And the new stove will be something we'll all share. I'm real proud of you, Serilda, not wanting to keep it all for yourself."

"Let's go to the post office first and get the letter, then we'll do the buying." Serilda sat up straight, little tingles running all over. This was going to be the best day she could remember. Locket coming home and buying all the new things.

But there wasn't any letter at the post office. Serilda asked the clerk to look twice to be sure. She turned away, sick with disappointment.

"It didn't say the letter would be here today. 'Follows' could mean anytime, might even be next week," Pa said as he drove to the hitchrack and tied the team.

"But the fair starts a week from Thursday, and I *have* to have the buggy!"

"A week can be a long time. Let's go look at the cookstoves."

They looked at the cookstoves and had another look at the buggies and the harness. There was still time left for a little visit with Katie, who told the wonderful news that there would be no classes on account of the fair and she could have the time off from Thursday morning until Sunday afternoon.

The train was over an hour late and Serilda waited in the wagon while Pa walked up town and bought some crackers and cheese and two thick slices of bologna. It was so tasty. Then back to the station. Pa sat down inside, but Serilda stayed outside looking down the track to the east. Would Locket be terrified after the all-day trip with whistles blowing, the train swaying, stopping, starting? Shut in the moving room all by herself, not knowing where she was going? Serilda traveled all the long worrisome miles in her mind.

It grew dusk, then dark. Finally out of the east came a long, mournful whistle and a sliver of light pierced the darkness. With a rumble and roar the train pulled into the station. Bells clanged, steam hissed from the engine. Voices yelled.

Serilda could hardly breathe. The conductor stepped off and waved a piece of paper in his hand. "Is Miss Serilda . . . ?"

"Here I am!" Serilda called and ran to him.

"Got orders to deliver a black horse to you. She's in the baggage car in a temporary stall. Pretty special, came first class. You're to sign this when you see if she is in good shape."

The door was pushed back. Bags, trunks, boxes and a sack of mail came first. Then a cleated ramp was hooked below the door and let down. "Stand back! Stand back! We're bringing out a horse!" the baggageman shouted.

The people moved back, but Serilda crowded close. Pa stood by the ramp. A man appeared, leading Locket. Serilda cried out. Every leg was bandaged to the knee. Something had happened as it had to Princess! Only worse.

"Oh, Locket, Locket! I'm here. See, I'm right here!" Locket gave a snort and rolled her eyes as she looked at the ramp, but when the man stepped on it she followed him down. The crowd cheered and moved farther back. "There's a note tied to her halter," the man said. "Mebbe you'd best read it now."

Pa untied it and Serilda read it quickly:

Take off bandages as soon as she arrives. They were only for protection while standing and riding so long. She left here in tip-top shape. Fine little show girl.

Boson

Pa ran his hands over Locket. "She's scared and shaking, but fit as a fiddle, far as I can tell." Serilda gave a deep sigh of relief and signed the paper.

At the town well, Pa took a bucket from the wagon and

gave all the horses a good cool drink. There they took off the bandages and rubbed Locket's legs.

Out of town it was cool and quiet. A full moon lighted the way. Tib and Tony, anxious to get home, wanted to trot, but Pa held them back for Locket was stiff and tired. When they were almost home Locket threw up her head and whinnied high and strong, again and again. Up in the pasture came Star's answering whinny and the sound of galloping hooves.

And down by the bridge came the sound of other whinnies as a camper's horses answered the call of their own kind.

"We'll leave Locket in the barn for tonight," Pa said as they unhitched and led the horses through the gate. "She's all tuckered out and it will feel good to rest her bones on a straw bed."

Serilda was tired, too, and she awoke later with a start, the high, shrill scream of fighting horses in her ears.

"Serilda!" Pa yelled from the bedroom. "Quick! Something's after the horses!"

The lamp shone suddenly on the table, showing Ma's tense face. Serilda jerked on her shoes and ran for the door as Pa grabbed his gun and came after.

It was moonlight. For a second they stood, horrified by the sight. The barn lot seemed filled with screaming, kicking, plunging horses in a cloud of dust! Grover barked savagely, dodging in and out.

Serilda heard Star's shrill neigh and the high, thin whinny of Teka. It seemed to come from the very center of the fighting. Serilda screamed and started toward them.

"Stop! Stay out of there!" Pa yelled and grabbed her arm. "Open the gate wide, then get out of the way. Quick! I'll go around on the other side and shoot in the air and try to stampede 'em!"

The gate was partly open and Serilda dragged it wide. She climbed up high on the fence. A shot rang out!

Suddenly a horse galloped into the yard and a man jumped down. "Don't shoot 'em! Don't shoot 'em!" he yelled and ran toward the milling horses, a coiled rope in his hand.

"He won't kill 'em! He's trying to scare 'em!" Serilda shouted.

A strange horse plunged out through the gate and ran toward the road. Pa yelled and shot again and two more ran through the gate, but a gray horse was left and he screamed a challenge and plunged toward a big dark horse. The big horse whirled and kicked and Serilda heard the hard thud when the hooves hit. Tib and Tony could fight too.

The stranger climbed on the fence by Serilda and stood on the top rail. He whirled the rope above his head and when the gray horse reared, the rope cut through the air and fell around its neck. The stranger jumped to the ground and hitched the rope around the post.

Serilda found her breath. "Pa! Come! Help! The man's got him. He roped him!"

The stranger got the horse over to the fence and through the gate. Serilda jumped down and shut the gate behind them. He was a little gray stallion and his eyes shone wild and fiery. He kicked and snorted and shook at the rope around his neck.

"He's a wild booger. Traded for him last week. Mustang. Folks glad to be rid of him, but I'll gentle him, give me time." The man stuck out his hand as Pa walked up. "I'm Bill Roberts, travelin' horsetrader. Me and my family camped down by the bridge this evenin', but the bunch heard your horses whinnyin' and broke loose. Sure thank you for jest shootin' in the air."

"I can't figger out how they got inside the barn lot. I know I shut the gate," Pa said, puzzled.

"I can figger. This gray scalawag can open any gate unless it's wired or padlocked. One o' the reasons I got him so cheap."

A horse whinnied up the road, and the stranger untied the stallion and got into the saddle. "Guess I'd better round up the others before they get into the next county. Sorry to cause all this trouble." And the mustang, knowing the fight was over, followed on the rope.

"Pa, I want to look at Star and Teka. They were right in the middle of the fight."

"Run and get the lantern. We'll look at Tib and Tony, too."

Tib and Tony were still prancing around the lot, wild-eyed, snorting and whinnying. Star was over in one corner with Teka behind her, head high, watching the road. From inside the barn came Locket's high excited whinny.

Except for a few welts and a small cut on Tony's neck, they were unhurt. Star was trembling. There was a hard welt on her shoulder and she flinched when Pa touched it. Serilda stooped to feel of Star's legs and gave a sharp cry.

"Oh, Pa, her leg's hurt. It's cut and bleeding awful."

It was a mean wound. A deep cut, curved like a hoof and as long as Pa's finger, cut across the old scar. Blood streamed across the white hair and made a dark blot in the dust. Pa pressed his fingers beside the cut and Star stepped uneasily.

"Lucky no bones broken, but it's cut clear down to the bone." Pa shook his head. Serilda blinked back the tears. Teka was unhurt.

They led Star into the yard and Ma brought out a pan of warm water and clean cloths. Serilda stood by Star's head while Pa washed out the wound and bandaged it.

"We'll put Star and Teka in the barn with Locket," Pa said as he tore off a strip of cloth and tied it around the bandage. "Turn Tib and Tony out into the pasture with the other stock."

There was a worrisome ache in Serilda's heart. "Pa, how long do you think it will be before Star's leg is healed?"

Pa leaned back on his heels and looked up at Serilda. "If you're wonderin' if she'll be well enough for the fair, she won't be. She'll have to stay home this year. The less she uses this leg the better for a month or more. Let's just be thankful it didn't break her leg."

Serilda shuddered and turned toward the barn, Star limping along beside her. Inside she threw her arms around Star's neck. "Don't you worry about missing the fair. Locket and I will bring you a blue ribbon," she whispered close against Star's face.

13

FAIRTIME

Early Monday morning when Charley Denton stopped by on his way to Chillicothe, Pa asked him to go by the post office and bring the mail. Charley was back by noon and reported there was no mail for the Shaws. On Tuesday another neighbor reported the same thing.

Wednesday morning, the day before the fair began, Pa and Serilda drove into town, sure that by now Serilda would hear from Mr. Bell. Serilda went to the little window herself to get the letter. The postmaster looked carefully, then shook his head.

"Do letters ever get lost?" Serilda asked.

"Very seldom. Maybe it has never been written," the postmaster suggested. Serilda turned away.

Pa was waiting in the buggy. They sat for a moment without talking and all the worry began again.

"I think Mr. Bell is honest, the money will come, but maybe not in time for the fair. Daughter, your Ma and I have talked it over and we'll loan you the money, to buy the new buggy and harness, or you can use your fifty-two dollars and owe Mr. Pringle for the balance until your letter comes."

"But if I didn't get the letter from Mr. Bell, with Star hurt, I might not get any fair money. Pa, you've always preached not ever to go in debt for things you didn't actually need, and could get along without." Serilda gave a long sigh. "I don't really need the new buggy. I just want it awful bad."

Twice Star had been shown at the fair hitched to the old buggy that squeaked and rattled more than ever this year. And for the first time Locket was to be shown in the ring as the best filly under three years. Serilda could almost see the shining filly parading back and forth and around the ring hitched to the new buggy. A new buggy and new harness might make the difference between first and second place. Better horses and more new buggies were appearing every year.

"Pa, the horses aren't shown till Friday. Let's wait. I've a feeling the letter will come tomorrow. Let's go and pick out the buggy and see if Mr. Pringle will hold it, then we can get it in a hurry when the letter comes."

So they went over to the carriage and wagon factory. There on the floor in the show window was *the* buggy. Red wheels, shiny black body, leather seat and cushion and the leather top that folded down. And in a little place under the seat, the oilcloth curtains neatly folded.

Mr. Pringle, himself, came to wait on them. "Of course I'll hold the buggy for you, but why not take it out today if you want it. You can pay part of it, the rest later. A Shaw's word is as good as a bond."

Serilda shook her head. "I'd rather pay the cash."

"Just step up into the buggy and feel the comfort of the cushions. Nice wide seat, plenty of leg room for a tall person. I've seen your sorrel mare and watched that black filly at the circus. The whole county is proud of them. Miss Serilda, you've some of the finest horses in the state and a buggy like this will set them off." Mr. Pringle was a good salesman.

Serilda stepped up into the buggy. She settled back in the seat. Pride swept over her. She picked up imaginary lines and drove right out of the showroom and into the fair-grounds. Not a squeak, not a rattle, as Locket paraded.

"Well, what do you think? Want to take it today? Fair starts tomorrow, you know?" Mr. Pringle broke into Serilda's dreaming. "And since it's you, we'll throw in a fancy summer laprobe, along with the whip."

"Oh, Mr. Pringle, I never use a whip."

"No? Take it anyway. Something about a whip that sets off a stylish rig like this."

Serilda hesitated. She'd heard Pa tell of folks who couldn't pay their debts and how it shamed them. Even if she owed Pa she'd want to pay him right away, same as Mr. Pringle. Surely the letter would come tomorrow, or the next day. But what if it didn't?

"I'll wait, Mr. Pringle, but if I want it in a hurry, can I get it quick?"

Mr. Pringle looked puzzled. "Of course, in five minutes, but why not take it now?" He looked at Pa.

Pa shook his head. "Anything to do with her horses, I

Serilda settled back in the seat, picked up imaginary lines

never give advice, unless she asks me. That's our agreement."

As they started home, Serilda choked back her disappointment. Star hurt and no letter from Mr. Bell, everything seemed to be going wrong.

At home Serilda put on a pair of Jeff's jeans and began washing the old buggy and shining it with beeswax. If she had to use it she would make it look as nice as she could. She rubbed and polished with fierce determination. Pa and little Bill went to the field to get the pumpkin Pa had been watching all summer.

After the buggy was washed, Serilda put fresh bandages on Star's leg. It didn't seem to be healing as fast as it should and Grandma said to use some of the herb salve. It didn't really seem like fairtime with so many things to worry about.

Ma and Grandma were busy cooking and baking. This year Ma was going to enter one of her vinegar pies that everybody bragged about.

At last everything was ready. Corn shucked and silked, apples polished, a fine, crisp cabbage head, a huge crook-necked squash and the big pumpkin washed and clean. Even a big striped gourd was to be entered. Grandma's new quilt and Ma's coverlid were wrapped in clean pillowcases. A special loaf of bread, baked in a pan by itself, and the vinegar pie waited in the cupboard. The Shaws would be well represented at the fair, not counting the horses. It had been a long day.

Pa was up before daylight, singing as he went to the barn. People were already going by, cows bawled, and calves bleated as they were taken along. This was the day for cattle and oxen to be shown and all exhibits entered.

Ma and Pa left early, driving Tib and Tony. The garden things rested on a bed of straw in the back of the wagon, but Ma put the loaf of bread between them on the seat and held the vinegar pie carefully on her lap. Pa was going by the post office and would come home early if the letter was there. Katie was coming home with them, too.

Serilda watched them go until they were out of sight. Grover stood beside her and nosed her hand. In the kitchen Grandma and little Bill were talking. She turned and looked across the valley to the blue of Indian Hill, then up in the pasture where Star was grazing. It would seem strange not to drive Star at the fair. Who would get the blue ribbon for best driving horse? Colonel Thompson did not plan to enter Black Chief. Last year a horse from down toward Lexington had made Star work hard for the ribbon. The Chillicothe fair was known everywhere and more people came every year and entered exhibits and showed horses and livestock.

Suddenly Locket whinnied. Serilda laughed and ran toward the barn. She had a feeling Pa would bring the letter and Katie would be with them. She hitched Locket to the buggy and drove to the pasture. They had practiced driving before, time after time, but Locket had ideas of her own about turning and pulling a buggy. Sometimes she wanted to pull and sometimes she didn't, and the turning she disliked most of all. Serilda riding her was different, she liked that, and doing tricks was the very best.

It was midafternoon when Serilda heard the rumble of the wagon and ran to the yard to meet Katie and the folks. She hummed a happy little tune. So much to tell Katie and all the plans for tomorrow.

But Pa and Ma were alone. Serilda ran to the wagon. "Where's Katie?"

"We went by to get her, but the Beaucamps had a houseful of folks for dinner and Katie thought she should stay and help. She will get off tomorrow and Saturday for sure."

Serilda felt a tightness in her throat. "And the letter? Pa, you've got the letter?"

Pa got down from the wagon before he answered. "No, daughter the letter hadn't come. The postmaster said one more train would be in this evening and it might come on that. He felt real sorry about it, same as Ma and me."

Ma got down from the wagon. "We saw Colonel Thompson and he was sorry to hear about Star, said folks would miss her at the fair." Ma put her hand on Serilda's shoulder and her voice made a lump come in Serilda's throat.

"Pa and me talked coming home, as Pa told you before. If you want to use some of the house money we've saved to get your buggy, we can use the buggy, too."

"Ma, you've wanted the new house ever since I could remember and done without things: a spring wagon, or a surrey or a stove. You'd rather have any one of those things than a buggy. I know. And maybe I wouldn't get enough money to pay it back for years!"

"Don't feel so hurt, Serilda," Pa said. "You've got the contract that Mr. Bell signed. You'll get the money sometime, even though it may take years to do it. The law is on your side."

"But I don't want to go to law," Serilda said brokenly. "I like India and Boson and Mr. Bell."

As they sat around the supper table, Serilda couldn't talk. For the first time she began to doubt the Bells. She thought of borrowing the money at the bank. She'd rather owe the bank than Pa or Mr. Pringle. Then she pushed the thought aside. She'd use the old buggy. She wouldn't owe anybody! Star lame, Katie and Jeff gone. It didn't seem like fairtime at all.

Outside, wagons and horseback riders were going home from the fair and one of them stopped in the road and Serilda heard voices. Then there were footsteps in the yard and Pa stepped to the door. He smiled all over his face. "Well, look who's here!" And in walked Katie, smiling at everybody.

"The company left and I went up town to see if I could catch a ride and found the Dentons." She opened her reticule and took out an envelope. "And, Serilda, I went by the post office the last thing and the train had come in and there was a letter for you. From Hannibal. And look, on the outside it says, *"Missent to Quincy, Illinois!"*

Serilda suddenly felt lighter than air. She grabbed Katie and hugged her so tight she choked. Then she tore open the envelope and took out a folded sheet of paper with another piece of paper fastened to it. "Bank draft," Serilda read aloud, "for two hundred and fifty dollars, on the First National Bank of Hannibal, and signed—Samuel W. Bell."

"Good as gold," Pa said and there was relief in his voice. It was a short letter.

Dear Serilda:

We are very happy to send payment for services performed by your little filly, Locket. She was quite a drawing card and most satisfactory.

The offer I made you a few weeks ago still stands. Please let me know at once if Locket arrived safely and also if draft is received in good order.

India and Boson send love and best wishes and Mrs. Bell asks to be remembered to your mother.

Sincerely,
Samuel W. Bell

Serilda grabbed Katie again and danced her around the kitchen. "Oh, Katie, I thank you a trillion times and I'll write to Mr. Bell right this minute so we can mail it tomorrow."

She hurried to get the pen and paper. It would be an easy letter to write.

14

LOCKET AT THE FAIR

In the morning breakfast was hurried and by seven o'clock the Shaws were on their way. Serilda had checked everything, saddle, saddle blanket, currycomb, brush and rubrags, the locket Katie had loaned her was around her neck and the bank draft in the reticule on her arm.

Pa looked handsome driving Tib and Tony, and Ma beside him was as pretty as any girl. Grandma had on the new gray silk Aunt Matilda had brought from Boston and Ma had made. Katie had on one of the new school dresses and Serilda wore a new one, too. Even little Bill had on new copper-toed shoes. The Shaws were looking their very best. And Locket, prancing along behind the wagon, was as sleek and stylish as a fine lady.

It's my kind of day, Serilda thought as she looked at the bright blue sky with cottony clouds. Not far away the Knob, highest of all the hills in the county, was colored with the red and gold of autumn. Persimmons hung thick on bare-limbed trees. Back in the woods a wild turkey gobbled and a covey of quails ran in front of the team for a little way, then flew with a whir into the pasture. A meadowlark sang to them from a fence rail.

But there was a little ache, too, in Serilda's heart. Jeff wouldn't be at the fair. Every year he had helped to get Star ready to show and was there to help celebrate when she won. And Star would not be there, either. Home with a bandaged leg, limping around the pasture, the blue ribbon she might have won would be given to some other horse. Serilda gave a little sigh. Then she looked at Locket and tried to push aside her worries. Locket just had to win the ribbon! It would be fun to tell Jeff all about the fair and everything that happened. A thrill of expectation ran over her.

As they neared town, teams and wagons and buggies crowded the road. The dust grew thicker, it never had time to settle. Neighbors called out to them and they called back. It was a gay time. Pa sat up a little straighter and Ma's face was pink.

Pa tied the team in front of the bank and he and Serilda went inside. The cashier at the window looked at the draft, peered a little closer, turned it over and then smiled. "It's perfectly good, Miss Serilda. Sign your name right here." He handed a pen through the window.

Then he counted out ten twenty-dollar gold pieces, three ten-dollar gold pieces and four five-dollar gold pieces and pushed them out in front of Serilda. Carefully she picked them up and put them in her reticule. It sagged with the weight of them.

She tried to walk sedately beside Pa as they went to the

carriage factory, but she felt as if she were floating along, her feet barely touching the boards in the sidewalk. She held the reticule tightly, the weight of it on her arm a lovely reminder.

Mr. Pringle came to meet them.

"I came for my buggy. Can I have it right now?"

"You bet. This very minute. We'll pull it out in front so you can hitch your horse to it. And here's the whip and lap-robe, compliments of Stafford and Pringle."

Serilda carefully counted out the money and Mr. Pringle smiled as he picked it up. "I see you have the cash, and I thank you very much, Miss Serilda. Would you like the top up or down?"

"Down, please."

"I'll get Locket," Pa said and started out of the door; then he turned, a funny little grin on his face. "We're getting the cart before the horse for sure. Serilda, we have to buy the harness." They all laughed. Getting so many new things all at once was enough to get anybody flustered.

It was not far to the harness shop. The harness Serilda had chosen was there on its peg. Black leather and hand-stitched, it was a beautiful set. The bridle was without blinders and on each side of the headband were silver buttons with the head of a horse embossed, and red tassels hanging down. Pa said it was the finest set of single harness he'd ever seen. Serilda bought it and Pa carried it back to the wagon. The reticule was rapidly getting lighter.

Pa drove around to the front of the factory and Katie got out to help. The harness was put on Locket and adjusted to her. But Locket wasn't sure that she enjoyed the feel of it. She pranced and pawed and shook her head.

Pa helped Serilda and Katie into the buggy as if they had been grownups. "We'll see you at the fair," he said as he handed Serilda the lines and spread the laprobe over their knees. He gave Locket a pat and stepped aside, a proud look on his face.

Locket was excited, she pulled at the bit and wanted to get away. It was the first time she had ever been in town hitched to a buggy and you could tell she didn't like the strangeness. Serilda talked and held her back and tried to quiet her. They got in a line of buggies and carts and wagons that went slowly toward the fairgrounds. But Locket chewed on the new bit, pranced and sidestepped until she was wet with sweat. "Katie, do you think she'll settle down by show time?" Serilda was worried.

"The harness is stiff and feels strange and the buggy behind her looks different, bigger, shinier, heavier and has a top. As new shoes feel to us, maybe. It's too bad she didn't have time to get used to it." Katie was worried, too.

They were close now to the fairgrounds. The muted sound of the band came to them, the strange lovely smell of the fair and the murmur of hundreds of voices. Serilda felt excitement wash over her.

A sudden yell stopped them. It was Jeff, shouting and waving. He came running and climbed into the buggy.

"I didn't know you at first. Made my eyes bug out. Locket looks so frizzlin' fine in her new harness and the new buggy.

Didn't think I was going to get here, but Steve said I could work a day extra to make it up. Caught a ride in, but have to go back tonight. Katie, don't you have to go to school? Where's Pa and Ma? And say . . . where's Star?"

They all talked at once.

They found a shady spot near the show ring and unhitched Locket and tied her to the tree. They admired every inch of the new buggy and harness, but Locket looked as if she was glad to be rid of it.

The folks came soon, and Pa and Serilda hurried to register and pay the fee. In less than an hour Pa would be showing Tib and Tony in the draft horse class. Jeff and Pa each grabbed a rubrag and went to work on the big bays. Serilda and Katie dusted the wagon and wiped off the harness. Everything was shining. The whole family was standing together, watching, when Pa drove into the ring.

"The horses get bigger and better every year," Jeff said worriedly as a handsome team of dapple grays came in behind Pa.

"Best team of draft horses, shown by owner," the announcer called out through his shiny tin horn. "Drive once around the ring."

"Look at that pair of sorrels!" Serilda said. "Where do they come from. Never see 'em on Saturdays."

"Mr. Beaucamp said farmers who could afford it were getting heavy work horses instead of oxen," Katie said.

Ma and Grandma stood quiet, watching, even little Bill was quiet. Serilda leaned against the rope, making every turn and move with Pa. Around the ring Tib and Tony walked briskly, solidly, trotting when Pa gave the word, moving as one horse, ears forward, great necks arched. Serilda was as proud as Pa.

"Outside of that circus I never saw three such fine teams," Jeff whispered as they went around the ring for the final time.

"Line up your teams before the judges' stand," came the command. The horses were unhitched and examined carefully, then hitched again. The dapple grays, the sorrels, and Tib and Tony were motioned around the ring again. These were the three best. Serilda could hardly breathe as she watched the judges.

"It will be close," Jeff whispered.

Then they were lined up again, and the judge walked out with two blue ribbons and fastened one on the sorrels and the other on Pa's Tib and Tony!

"After careful consideration, the judges decided on two awards. A blue ribbon and ten dollars in gold to Will Shaw of Livingston County, and a blue ribbon and ten dollars in gold to George Randolph of Linn County, who tied for first place with their full-blooded Percherons."

The Shaw family let out a long breath of relief. "Do you think it will be that tough for Locket?" Serilda asked as they hurried back to the wagon. "I wish there had been more time to get her used to the new things."

There was no time to wonder and worry. The family ate their dinner and the horses were fed and watered. The under three-year-olds were next on the list. Locket was given a final polish, then she was hitched to the buggy, the sidesaddle, saddle blanket and bridle put in the back.

Serilda pulled on the long riding skirt. This was going to be hard, driving, then changing to riding and back again to driving. As she started to climb into the buggy, Ma stopped her, smoothed her hair and straightened her bonnet and wiped a smudge from her face. "I do declare, Serilda, you worry and work on the horses and never give a mind to yourself."

Serilda smiled absently at Ma, climbed in and picked up the lines.

"Everything is fine," Katie said as she gave Locket a pat.

Serilda was the last one to drive in. Four others were already driving around the ring. Two bays, one of them big and rangy, driven by a man Serilda recognized. Last year Star had won against a bay mare he drove. There was a neat little sorrel and a shining dapple gray hitched to a rattling old buckboard, the driver a boy about Serilda's age, sitting on a folded quilt. Then there was Locket hitched to the new buggy. Serilda was the only girl.

The announcer picked up his horn. "All entries are under three years old, shown by owner, and broken to drive and ride. Walk your horses around the ring."

Single file they started around, the big rangy bay leading.

15

A BLUE RIBBON

Locket tossed her head. She sidestepped and shied when a boy popped a paper sack. She pulled at the bit and pranced. She did not like being held back. She acted as if she had never seen a crowd before or performed in a circus and ridden on a train. Serilda spoke softly, trying to quiet her. Driving her was not as easy as driving Star who knew all the tricks and turns. These horses were all young and inexperienced, their first time in the ring. Serilda glanced ahead, others were having their troubles, too. Twice around the ring they walked their horses.

"Trot your horses!"

Serilda loosened the lines and Locket began to trot, free and high-stepping, neck bowed and her tail arched. All at once Serilda felt gay and sure. This was almost as good as Star could do. Once around the ring and the crowd clapped as they went by. Serilda loosened the lines a bit more and Locket increased her speed. She passed the little bay and the sorrel, then she passed the rangy bay whose driver was having a hard time managing the nervous, high-strung horse.

Serilda was glad to be around him. Ahead the boy on the buckboard sat on his quilt, driving the dapple gray.

Then without warning there was a sudden rush and the bay was pounding up beside them, snorting, plunging, galloping out of control, the driver sawing on the lines, the wheels of the buggies only inches apart!

For a second Serilda froze with horror. Then she gasped and slapped Locket with the lines. "Go! Locket! Go!" she cried out. Locket laid back her ears, she stretched out low to the ground, a flying black filly that split the wind! The buggy slithered around the turn. They were out ahead!

Behind them the driver yelled as the bay plunged into the ropes. People screamed and shouted. Serilda dared not look as she pulled on the lines and tried to stop, but Locket was frightened by the rearing horse and yelling people.

Serilda was frightened, too, but she braced her feet and kept a steady pull on the lines. She talked to Locket, saying her name over and over, but they went around the ring again before Serilda could slow her down and get in line before the judges' stand.

Locket was breathing hard, flanks trembling, and sweat running in dark streams on her body, flecks of foam on her neck. Serilda wished they could rest a moment, for the showing was only half over. She glanced at the rangy bay being led from the ring, a worried frown on her face. This was the first time a horse had ever gotten out of control in the ring.

"Change to saddle and walk your horses."

Serilda pulled up the long riding skirt, jumped down from

the buggy and began unhitching Locket, but the new harness was stiff and hard to manage. She tried to hurry, but her fingers were numb from gripping the lines. Locket was nervous and kept sidestepping. No help was allowed except to mount.

At last the harness was off, the saddle on, and one of the judges gave Serilda his hand to mount. Next to her the boy on the buckboard had put the folded quilt on his horse, fastened it with a surcingle, sprang up and was halfway around the ring. Serilda glanced at him enviously as she settled herself on the sidesaddle and arranged her skirt.

Locket was still excited. Serilda could feel her tremble. She reached over and patted her neck and talked to her.

"Come on, Locket, let's forget the poor scared bay and show 'em what a really fine saddle horse you are."

As she walked around the ring, Locket quieted. She cantered and trotted and changed gaits like an old-timer, her white foot flashing. "This is fun," every line of her trim body announced.

"Choose your gait."

This was what Serilda had been waiting for. Locket began single-footing, swift and smooth and easy. Serilda hardly moved in the saddle. She felt as if she and Locket were all one being, gay and free as the birds. At this Locket was perfect and she loved to do it.

Then suddenly trouble exploded! Across the ring came a howling, yiping dog, chased by a pack of dogs that came tearing straight toward them. The sorrel reared as they passed her and suddenly the snarling, barking tangle of dogs

Then suddenly trouble exploded!

erupted at Locket's feet. People shouted! A man came running!

Serilda cried out and grabbed Locket's mane. All in a breath Locket gave a wild snort and sailed in a flying leap over the dogs. She snorted again and kicked out as she landed, then she broke into a hard gallop, passing the boy on the dapple gray.

Serilda tried to talk to Locket, but the words stuck in her throat. Her bonnet hung down her back. Her heart pounded. She tried to sit straight in the saddle, but her back felt limp. How could she ever get Locket harnessed and hitched to the buggy again?

"Back into harness, around the track and line up for the judges."

As Serilda slid to the ground she felt as if her knees would fold. She leaned her head against Locket for a moment, and as if she needed comfort, too, Locket turned her head and rubbed her nose against Serilda. "The blue ribbon is gone, Locket," Serilda whispered brokenly, "but you did your very best."

She took off the saddle, put on the harness and finally got Locket hitched to the buggy. She was hot and tired and the last one to get started, but she petted Locket for a moment before she took the lines and climbed into the buggy. Some of the others had already been around the ring and were lined up for the judges.

As they started around, Serilda heard little Bill's high, shrill voice. "Sing and clap, Serilda! Sing and clap!" She turned toward the voice and saw Pa holding little Bill on his shoulder, the others close around him. Jeff and Katie waved. The crowd laughed, and some of them cheered.

It was what Serilda needed. She lifted her chin and spoke to Locket. She would not give up! She sat straight and put Locket into a trot. "This is your last chance," Serilda said softly, urgently. "Do your very best, Locket. Your very, very best."

And Locket did her very best. Smiling a little, Serilda lined up beside the dapple gray. There would be no blue ribbon this time, but there was a small chance for the red one. The judges walked around them. Colonel Thompson was with them this time, smiling and tipping his hat to Serilda. The judges frowned and could not agree.

"The black and the gray once more around, turn right and back in line."

It must be for second place, Serilda thought tiredly as they started around. A new buggy and harness and the best horse of all and she and Locket could be beaten by a boy on a buckboard sitting on an old quilt. And for second place, too!

They lined up again and Locket took her stand beside the dapple gray. Serilda stared straight ahead, even if they gave the red ribbon to the gray horse, she would not let on. She squared her shoulders.

"Ladies and Gentlemen!" the announcer called out. "We wish to call attention to these fine young horses. All under three years. Except for the big bay that had bad luck, all of the entries are colts by Black Chief, the famous Thoroughbred owned by Colonel Thompson and many times a blue-ribbon winner. We have asked Colonel Thompson to present the awards. First place and ten dollars in gold goes to Locket, owned and shown by Miss Serilda Shaw. Congratulations, Miss Serilda, for a fine filly and for the way the pair of you managed two serious situations."

Serilda was shocked with amazement. Colonel Thompson smiled as he handed her the blue ribbon and the little box.

"It was close, Miss Serilda, but under the saddle Locket is the best two-year old I ever saw." He stepped a little nearer and lowered his voice. "And the speed she put on to get away from the tight place and the jump over the dog fight didn't hinder. It showed what she could do when pressed to it."

Serilda looked at him in unbelief. She nodded her thanks, her heart too full to speak.

"Second prize and five dollars in gold goes to David Green." The Colonel handed the red ribbon and a box to the boy on the buckboard who came so very near being first.

David took the box and the ribbon and thanked the Colonel. Then he looked up at Serilda. "This year I got the red one, but next year I'll take the blue. I'm warning you."

Serilda laughed and found her voice. "You'll have to work mighty hard if you do." For the first time she really looked at the dapple gray, sleek and shining and alert. "You do have a fine horse," she said admiringly.

"Once around the ring, winner lead out!"

It was a proud moment and Locket knew it. She led the line in a swift high-stepping trot, the new buggy glistened in the sunshine, the harness shone with a soft luster. Serilda fairly tingled with excitement and joy. It sang in her heart and flowed down the lines to Locket. The dog fight, the bee stings, the tiredness, the weeks of worry were all swept away. She wished the family could be right beside her in the buggy riding around the ring! And Star, too!

Jeff met her at the entrance. He jumped in the buggy.

"Golly, were we scared when that big bay got to crowding you! Thought sure you'd go into the ropes. Ma almost fainted and Grandma prayed right out loud. You might have been killed! And then the dog fight! Serilda, it's as hard on us watching as it is you driving!" Jeff wiped the sweat from his face.

It was a blue-ribbon day for the whole Shaw family. Ma won first on the vinegar pie, but Lisa Denton won the blue ribbon for her new coverlid, Ma the red one. Grandma and a woman up Poosey-way shared honors for best quilt and Pa got first for the biggest pumpkin.

The next morning, Ma said two days hand-running at the fair was enough for her and that she was staying at home to churn and bake bread and catch up on the work. Grandma and little Bill elected to stay with her. That suited Serilda and Pa just fine, for after picking up the exhibits at the fair they had important business to attend to.

So Serilda and Katie and Pa took the Percherons and the wagon and went to the fair again and after two o'clock got the quilt and the coverlid and Pa's big pumpkin. Then they drove back to the hardware store and bought the cookstove that Ma had liked the best.

It had four lids on the top and at one end a door to put in the wood. The oven had doors on each side and Pa said two people could toast their feet at the same time. There was a hearth where Grandma could set the ironstone teapot to keep it warm. There was a damper, too, that controlled the heat in the oven or let it go up the chimney.

Serilda paid the cash and Pa and the clerk lifted the stove up into the wagon.

When they were started home, Serilda turned toward Katie and said the old rhyme:

"Hold out your hands and shut your eyes,
And I'll give you something to make you wise."

Katie smiled, shut her eyes, and held out her hands. Serilda put two twenty-dollar gold pieces on her palms. When Katie opened her eyes, she gasped and stared. "Forty dollars! Oh, Serilda, it's too much! It's too much!"

"It's for the seminary and books and things you'll need. And don't say it's too much. You earned every cent, helping train Locket and showing me all about horses!" Serilda said, trying to keep her voice steady.

Katie put her arms around Serilda and squeezed her tight, her eyes brimming with tears. Pa began to sing, loud and gusty.

The reticule was getting very light, but Serilda gave a pleased little smile when she hefted it.

It was a slow, careful drive home. Shadows stretched across the road and whippoorwills were calling as Pa drove into the yard and pulled up close to the back door to unload the stove.

Serilda and Katie hopped down and began taking out the

endgate. Then Ma came to the door. When she saw the stove, she stopped stone still, her eyes wide.

Pa spoke up. "Don't blame me, Ma, it's Serilda's doings. She set her mind that you should have a stove. She paid for it."

Ma turned to Serilda. Her lips moved, but no words came. She held out her arms and Serilda ran to her and they hugged each other tight, and suddenly they were laughing and crying together as if Ma were another girl. It was the best part of the whole week.

Jeff came home as they were eating supper, looking almost a man grown as he came into the house. He had bridge-money in his pocket, earned by his own labor. They sat around the table and talked until long after bedtime.

It was raining in the morning, but the sky cleared by noon, leaving the air as sparkling as fresh cider.

Serilda felt restless. Tomorrow she and Jeff would start their last year at Red Oaks school and Katie would be back in Chillicothe. She washed the last of the dinner dishes and turned to Katie.

"Let's get Jeff and run up to the rock for a little while before we take you back to school. No telling when we'll have another chance."

So they ran up the path to the flat rock on the high hill and climbed upon it, Grover barking and jumping up beside them. Star and Locket whinnied and started toward them, Teka running circles, even Tib and Tony began ambling that way.

The air was so clear that Indian Hill stood out sharp and

clean, a deep, dark blue against the sky. Flaming red and yellow trees, rain-washed, spread over the valley like a bright coverlid.

Down below they could see the roof of the covered bridge and the mill and the road that wound in and out among the trees. A thin wisp of smoke marked a camper's fire at the foot of the hill.

Serilda felt a strange loneliness in her heart, and a happiness, too, as she thought of all the times the three of them had sat here and talked and planned. Some of the plans had already come true. Katie in seminary, Jeff working on a bridge, the new buggy and harness and Locket's first blue ribbon.

Katie broke the silence. "I do believe this is the prettiest spot in all of creation."

"It sure is," Jeff said. "And this year seems it's just plumb outdone itself. Kinda dazzles your eyes."

Serilda took a long, deep satisfying breath. She threw her arms wide to take in everything she could see, the valley, the bridge, the log house, the horses, Jeff, Katie and even Grover, close against her. "It . . . it . . . dazzles your heart, too!" she said with a quick, gay lilt to her voice. "And if I live to be twice as old as Grandma, I'll not ever, ever forget it."

Jeff and Katie laughed and clapped their hands at such a speech and the horses threw up their heads and looked at them. Out over the valley a hawk sailed in widening circles and from far below came the faint rumble as a wagon crossed the covered bridge. It was a day to remember.

ABOUT THE AUTHOR

OLIVE RAMBO COOK was reared on a farm in northern Missouri and, for picnic excursions, there was an old mill and an old bridge. Often, at county fairs, she showed both riding and driving horses. She was allowed to ride her father's finest saddle horse. Her own horse was rough to ride and performed much better hitched to a buggy. Memories of her growing-up days include long Sunday walks over the farm. Her father allowed her to take on responsibilities the farm neighbors felt beyond her years, but she has always been grateful to him. There was the fun of staying overnight with neighbor girls, of ice-cream suppers at the little country church, of going to the one-room school, so like the one she used in her *Coon Holler*.

High school and a local college in Chillicothe were followed by work with the Campfire Girls and as a teacher. She is married and has a grown son.

Research for *Serilda's Star* included consulting a man who had actually worked on covered bridges; an old-timer described for her the forebay of the old mill where he had played as a boy; a woman, really named Serilda, told of her childhood days near the covered bridge. Best of all, Mrs. Cook's own grandmother, born in 1824, lived with them, so actually, she grew up knowing pioneer ways. That is why *Serilda's Star* has so many anecdotes that impart the flavor of that 1866–1868 period. And now with *Locket* we have a fine continuing story of Serilda and her family and friends. Another good story in which horses figure largely.